YOU HAD ME AT ICE CREAM

FROM TREADMILL TO TRUE LOVE?

ANGELA PEARSE
C.G. LAMBERT

First Paperback edition July 2023
Published by Clamp Ltd. (clamp.pub)

Set in Sabon and Futura
Cover art by Kostis Pavlou kostispavlou.com

ISBN 978-1-914531-39-2 Hardback (IS)

ISBN 978-1-914531-40-8 Paperback (IS)

ISBN 978-1-914531-41-5 Paperback (KDP)

For our mums

Chapter 1

ZARA

'Eight, nine, ten, eleven—you can do it!—twelve, thirteen ... you'll thank me later.' Zara smiled encouragingly.

'No, I won't,' Rebecca puffed, her red cheeks glistening with sweat. 'You're not the one down here doing crunches.'

She was on her second set and Zara blithely ignored the bitching and moaning. As her personal trainer, it was her job to help Rebecca fit into her wedding dress (bought on sale and slightly too tight) before she walked down the aisle in three weeks' time. They still had work to do before that was going to happen. Progress was slow since Rebecca insisted on eating a block of chocolate every two days because of 'wedding stress'.

Zara wasn't a magician, but she also wasn't a quitter. She believed in Rebecca; the hard part was getting Rebecca to believe in herself. Gym management liked them to have mottos to encourage client positivity, and luckily Zara had a few up her sleeve. 'Stick with the programme and you'll see the results' was usually a morale booster. Another favourite was 'Sore today, stronger tomorrow'.

However, Zara had been forced to trot out several others during the hour-long workout in an attempt to raise her client's confidence. They'd barely finished the warm-up when Rebecca had turned to her and wailed, 'This is pointless. I tried it on last night and I couldn't even do up the zip! At this rate, I'm going to be walking down the aisle in a bin liner. PLEASE HELP ME!'

As a result, Zara adjusted Rebecca's programme to include more cardio and crunches—a lot of them.

'Twenty-five, twenty-six …'

Jase chose that moment to saunter past, and Zara momentarily lost concentration. She hadn't heard from him for the past week as he'd been off-grid in Newquay with a bunch of his mates. *Damn,* she thought. *I knew I should've worn my Lululemon leggings today.*

Rebecca took advantage of the pause in her counting to stop crunching. They watched as blond-haired Jase sat down and started working out on one of the Cable Lat Pulldowns. The muscles in his tanned back and shoulders rippled under his tank top. It looked like he'd been making the most of the Cornish sun. 'Is he your boyfriend?' Rebecca whispered to Zara, sounding impressed. 'He's built.'

'No. He's a PT colleague. Take a breather. Have some water. Then we'll start from the beginning,' Zara said firmly.

She wasn't about to divulge anything about her and Jase's personal relationship to a client. Rebecca grumbled but did as she was told. Zara cast an eye in Jase's direction again and fiddled with her ponytail. She couldn't deny she'd missed that body. It was just a pity he didn't talk about anything other than the best protein powders on the market.

Zara finished up their session with some full body stretches and reassured Rebecca with 'together we'll make it happen'. She also gave her a hug since she'd done over one hundred crunches and would likely be feeling it tonight.

After a twenty-minute jog on the treadmill, Zara took a shower and headed to the lunch room for some food before her first afternoon client. Grabbing her chicken salad with a boiled egg and extra nuts out of the fridge, she turned around to find Jase leaning against the counter with his arms folded, watching her with the same intent gaze she'd used on him. He was now topless and covered in a light sheen of sweat that made his skin glisten. His muscles were bulging. *Nice gains,* she thought.

He gave her a slow nod and a grin. 'Zee.'

'Jase. So how was the camping?' she asked, sitting down at the table and trying not to gawk at his body. The shirtless wonder. She knew it was for her benefit; he was on the prowl and probably wanted to hook up tonight.

He shrugged. 'It was OK. Weather turned shite at the end

but we got in a decent amount of surfing and hiking. Speaking of exercise, are you free tonight? I can tell you all about it.'

OK, she thought, *he definitely wants to hook up.* 'Exercise' was his code for a horizontal workout. She wasn't against the sex, it was pretty great, but it was all sex with him and nothing else. It was niggling her a lot lately. She just wished they could go out and do something intellectually stimulating. Despite Zara's gym bunny appearance, she did have a brain, but Jase didn't feel the need to engage with it.

Opening her container, she took a forkful of chicken and lettuce and said nonchalantly, 'I was thinking of going to a movie. There's a rerun of *The Last of the Mohicans* playing at the Barbican Cinema at six-fifteen. You're welcome to come with.'

'Oh.' Jase unfolded his arms, looked at her closely, and then folded them again. He seemed at a loss for words. To be fair, this was the first time she'd suggested doing something out of the bedroom in the three months they'd been casually seeing each other. But he might've known this was coming. The last time they hooked up, she'd mentioned their relationship needed to *evolve or dissolve.*

He smiled unconvincingly. 'Sure, I'll go. Beats doing my washing.'

'You will?'

'Of course. Er, what's it about?'

'You'll love it, it's got guns and fighting and Indians,' Zara said. *Also, the sublime Daniel Day-Lewis, stalking around looking masculine and hot. Phwoar.*

'Great,' he replied. 'I'll meet you at the theatre after my last session.' With that arranged, Jase took down a tub of protein powder from the top cupboard, dumped a generous scoop in a tall glass and filled it with water from the water cooler. He gave it a vigorous stir so it swirled greenly. To Zara, the concoction looked disgusting.

'Urgh. What's that?'

'Kelp, fermented pea protein, spinach and banana.'

'Rather you than me.' She pinched her nostrils as the smell assailed them.

'It tastes better than it looks.' He took a deep swallow and flexed a bicep. 'I can feel it giving me strength already.'

She rolled her eyes. 'Sure, Popeye.'

He finished the rest in two gulps. 'Right, that's lunch. I've got a session in five, so I'd better put a top on. It's a yummy mummy trio, and I don't want to distract them.' He waggled his eyebrows. 'Laters.'

Zara nodded. 'See you.'

She was pleasantly surprised that Jase had stepped up to the mark. Who knew, he might reveal a different side to him. One that involved something more than muscle. It was highly unlikely, but she was reluctant to throw the brawny baby out with the bathwater; she'd give him a chance at least. After all, as she often told her clients: 'If you want something you've never had, you must be willing to do something you've never done.'

Chapter 2

OLIVER

Eight hundred and fifty stairs. Oliver stared at them, the path zigzagging up and out of view behind the rocky outcrops. The early morning breeze was chillier than he was used to, but he knew that once he got moving he would warm up, and then when the desert sun popped over the horizon it would get really hot. Best to scale the heights while it was still cool.

He had climbed the stairs to Monastery at Petra three years ago. It had taken him half an hour, bouncing from one step to the other, pausing only to briefly gaze at the view before bounding off ahead. It had been early in the morning as well, the tents along the path and their slumbering shopkeepers more often than not protected by a barking dog, the noise bouncing off the canyon walls and echoing into the valley below.

But that had been three years ago. Covid hadn't been kind to him. Working from home on a desk-based job had robbed him of his incidental exercise—walking from his office desk to the burrito van outside or to and from the Tube. And he wasn't an idiot: he knew that he would be stretching his current abilities going up the stairs. His ultramarathon friend Paul had told him that if he prepared with low-impact walking, at a level where you could hold a conversation, Oliver would be OK and gain fitness. So he'd done that for a month or so. It hadn't made any discernible difference to his fitness, and his Covid belly remained, but Paul was an ultramarathoner; surely he knew what he was on about?

Oliver was procrastinating. The Monastery above was not getting any closer. With a sigh, he hefted his daypack, heard the bottles of water sloshing inside, and headed off. He knew that not everyone made it up to the Monastery, many of the tourists were put off by how difficult the stairs were. But he had loved it so much that first time that he was adamant that he would see it again.

Halfway up, hands on knees and puffing like a steam train, he was cursing Paul. Mentally cursing, of course—he had no spare breath for anything. His preparation had been totally inadequate. Oliver just had no fitness at all. The extra weight around his midriff made his thighs burn with effort, and he had to rest every five minutes or so to regain his breath.

Those same tents which he had sprung past last time were showing more signs of life, the shopkeepers pinning the side flaps to the roof, exposing the cool interior and the uniform products: pewter camels, fridge magnets and beaded necklaces. The friendly lady storekeepers invited him in for tea, and Oliver waved them off exhausted, knowing that if he sat down, he would be hard-pressed to get going again.

Fortunately by now there were one or two other tourists on the trail, usually perfectly matching couples in different shades of khaki and beige, hiking trousers or shorts and wide-brimmed hats and the odd walking poles showing off the latest in trekking tech. The smiling women would bustle out to them to try and persuade them inside to take some tea or have a chat. Oliver guessed that when all the stores were selling the same thing, they had to differentiate themselves some other way. A welcoming smile and a cup of hot tea might do the trick.

It was hard work, but after an hour of relentless uphill trekking, Oliver managed to clamber down the few rocks to the wide-open area in front of the Monastery and bask in its glory while recovering his breath. An hour and a thousand photos later, he was ready to return. If he had paused to think about it, he would have realised it would be easier going down than it had been coming up. Sure, gravity helped, but the uneven surfaces and constant switchbacks still made it murder on his thighs.

The good news was that Oliver didn't need to stop quite

as often on the way down, but his legs still complained every step he took. And the longer he went down, the more tired he became and the less sure his footing was. He had to take exaggerated care in where he stepped, lest his plodding feet land less squarely on a step and either slip backwards, causing a barked shin or slip forward, hyperextending a knee.

Oliver had the end in sight when he met one of the local men, eyes smeared with kohl and wearing a thick jacket. Short at about five and a half feet tall with long hair, full beard, and a slight build, he was leading a line of donkeys up the steps. He looked Oliver up and down, noted the effort in which breathing took place and said in accented English, 'Yes, you could certainly do with the exercise.'

Oliver was too out of breath to retort angrily, and a range of responses flicked through his head. All sounded pensive and complaining. What was he going to say? *I used to be thin?* Or more accurately, *I used to be fit?* It really didn't matter what he *used* to be, did it?

Shrugging at the man's casual rudeness, Oliver headed slowly back towards the Treasury at the entrance to the complex, trying to stay in the shadows as much as possible. There was a long stretch of exposed path ahead of him, but off to the side, there was a smattering of tents perched in front of the cliffs, which provided a welcome respite from the sun. Each tent sold similar trinkets, and Oliver used the excuse of inspecting the wares of one of the shops to rest and cool down. He had entered as some of the other tourists were leaving, so it was just him and the shopkeeper, a taller local with the same long hair and beard as the guy who had commented on Oliver's fitness at the bottom of the stairs. Oliver avoided eye contact, wanting to relax in the coolness of the interior and not have the hard sell.

The shopkeeper called out, 'Welcome, can I help you with anything?'

Oliver kept looking at the pewter camels and assorted beads, totally indistinguishable from the same products in all the other stalls throughout the complex. 'Nah, I'm OK, thanks,' he murmured back.

There was a brief pause before the shopkeeper continued. 'Thank you,' he said. Oliver still didn't make eye contact, but his puzzlement must have shown because the shopkeeper explained: 'For responding.'

Oliver made sure to catch the shopkeeper's eye and gave him a nod as he left. At least he could treat him like a human, even if he wasn't in the market for a pewter trinket or harem pants with camels on them, he thought as he left the tent and embraced the heat.

Oliver made a vow to himself as he headed back towards the entrance to the complex, ignoring the flow of tourists, camels, donkeys, golf carts and local peoples as they swarmed this way and that around him. He'd been fit once, and while he hadn't been skinny, he certainly didn't have the paunch in front of him. When he got back to London, he would seriously look at doing something to get rid of it. But only once he was back in London: the hotel had a free chocolate tasting at five!

Chapter 3

ZARA

The Barbican Cinema wasn't too far away from the gym and since Zara lived in West Ealing, out in Zone Three, she didn't bother going home first. She'd brought a change of clothes and make-up with her, a habit formed from staying over at Jase's.

In hindsight, hooking up with Jase probably hadn't been the smartest decision she'd ever made. He was the hottest PT in the gym, so of course she'd noticed him, but she'd thought he wasn't interested as he'd only ever given her a friendly nod in passing. Then one afternoon, he'd offered to show her a series of glute exercises and had grasped her hips to make sure she was in the right position. She'd been pretty sure that was a come-on. Then the next day, he'd shared his protein bar with her and asked if she wanted to come over for an egg-white omelette that night, and she couldn't say no. They'd kept it under management's radar during work hours, and it was easy, things seemed to flow.

Now she shoved aside her misgivings about trying to take it to the next level. He'd agreed to come with her, surely that was a sign they were on the same page?

While she waited in the foyer for him to show up, she messaged her flatmate Erin to let her know she was going to the movies with Jase and could she please feed Lala two-thirds of a cup of cat biscuits. Lala was her eight-year-old Burmese who was currently on a strict diet. Erin didn't mind feeding her since she was home more often than not. Zara suspected Erin was actually pleased, as it meant she got the flat to herself and could watch musicals. Zara hated musicals. She was more into period dramas, romcoms and sci-fi.

Having a flatmate who was also your landlord could have been awkward. But Erin, a marketing exec who worked in Central London, was friendly, easygoing and, best of all, didn't mind her having Lala. She'd made sure to mention it when Erin first showed her the flat, in case it was a no-go having a pet.

'I should mention that I have a cat. If that's a problem, then I don't want to waste your time.'

But Erin had instantly brightened. 'Oooh, I love cats, what's its name?'

'Her name is Lala. Like the Teletubby—because she's well rounded.'

Erin had laughed. 'A PT with a fat cat. That's a first. You need to get her working out.'

'I can't get her to do anything. She's as stubborn as a mule, with the appetite of a lion.'

Erin had let out a snort. 'She sounds like my kind of cat.'

Zara had moved in immediately, and they'd got on well; she was pleased that Erin adored Lala. There was always the tiny niggle in the back of her mind that Erin could kick her out since she was the owner. But she couldn't foresee anything happening in the near future to ruin the arrangement.

Erin's message came through. *Sure. What the hell? You and Jase going to the movies! Don't tell me you're becoming a proper couple?*

Zara decided not to reply to that since Jase hadn't even shown up yet. He was pushing it, the movie started at six-fifteen and it was ten past. She was just about to buy her ticket and go in when he came strolling through the sliding door.

'There you are! I thought you'd forgotten.'

'Sorry, my client wanted to do some extra sets, and then I had to shower.'

His hair was wet and slicked back, and he smelt strongly of the gym's bathroom shower gel. He kissed her on the cheek and she relaxed a little. 'It's fine, let's just get our tickets and go in.'

'No rush, is there? Don't they always have lots of ads?'

'Not here. They might have one or two but then the movie starts. I don't want to miss the beginning.'

A steady stream of movie goers were getting their tickets checked and going through the cinema door. It was obviously a popular re-run and Zara really didn't want to get lumped with sitting in the first row. The *Last of the Mohicans* was a glorious middle-row cinematic experience, not a front-row crick-in-your-neck endurance. Plus she'd been looking forward to it for ages. She was beginning to wish she'd just come on her own. But it was too late now.

The seats they ended up getting weren't too bad, a third of the way back. Though once in the cinema, Jase insisted on going out to the foyer again to get popcorn. 'I burned a lot of calories today. And I didn't have my evening protein shake.'

He was out there for so long he missed most of the opening sequence, so Zara had to explain it to him in a series of stilted whispers. He did share his popcorn with her, and he'd bought her a Magnum, which appeased her since he knew she loved them. But fifteen minutes later, Jase had finished his snack and was fidgeting. 'How long is this?' he whispered.

'About two hours.'

'When does it start getting good?'

Zara fought back a spasm of annoyance and whispered, 'Just keep watching!' She should've known Jase's attention span was too minuscule to deal with this movie, especially after he'd mentioned he got bored during *Fast and Furious*. But he quietened down and seemed to be enjoying it, especially the shoot-out with the Indians. Caught up in the story, Zara forgot about Jase after a while, but then a tiny noise reached her ears, then a louder one. She whipped her head around to find Jase, head back on the seat, snoring with his mouth wide open. Mortified, she jabbed him sharply in the arm with her elbow.

He jerked awake at her prod. 'Wha? Wha?'

'You're snoring!' she whispered loudly.

'Sorry. It was a busy day.'

Everything was fine until the critical moment when Alice jumped off the cliff after her Indian lover, committing suicide rather than be without him. It was a powerful scene that always made Zara well up. *The poor girl, how terrible.* But then something even more terrible happened right next to her. Jase guffawed. Loudly. Zara turned with tears in her eyes to find him shaking with laughter.

'What the fuck is so funny?' she whispered. 'It's sad!'

'It's hilarious!' he whispered back. 'I can see why you like this movie.'

Zara took a deep, ragged breath and managed to stop herself from saying something she knew she'd regret later. From then on, Jase decided it was a comedy and kept chortling at all the poignant scenes and gagging at the romantic parts between Daniel Day-Lewis and Madeleine Stowe, which were *the best bits*!

She sat there tolerating his antics and fuming until the movie was finally over and the lights came on. He'd totally ruined it. What a cretin.

When they got outside, Jase was in a jovial mood.

'That was great. A larf and a half. So do you want to come back to mine for an evening workout?' Jase smirked and obviously thought that he was in with a chance.

Zara was so angry she couldn't speak. He was unbelievable. She just wanted to get the hell away from him.

'I'm going home,' she mumbled, rummaging in her bag for her Oyster card. 'I'll see you tomorrow.'

But Jase wasn't finished having his say. 'What's your problem? I went to the movie like you wanted. It was fun.'

Zara glared at him. 'A woman committing suicide isn't fun!'

'Oh, come on. You have to admit that bit was OTT.'

'If you can't see what's wrong with you laughing at that then you've got a major problem.'

'You obviously have no sense of humour.'

'Jase, I honestly think you've got a screw loose.'

He sighed and bit his lip, avoiding her eyes. 'Zee, listen, I don't think this is going to work. We've got different goals. I need someone who's more on board with my life philosophy.'

She stared at him, stunned. 'What life philosophy?' As far as she knew, Jase didn't plan more than two days in advance. And that usually just involved what protein shake he was going to consume.

'You know, the future and stuff. I don't think we should keep seeing each other.'

'You were fine with me coming round to your place five minutes ago!'

He shrugged. 'I don't think I can give you *more*. And I think we both know that's what you want.'

Zara's heart sank. He'd definitely taken on board her *evolve or dissolve* comment. Now he was dumping her. This was bad. Not only had she screwed the crew, but she would also see him all the time at the gym. She groaned inwardly.

A short time later, bumping along on the Elizabeth line to West Ealing, Zara was still in shock. Why had Jase even agreed to go to the movie if he was planning on breaking up? Why not just make up some excuse? Unless he'd decided to piss her off deliberately so he could play the 'see we're not right for each other' card. Yes, that was probably more like it.

Zara snorted in disgust, making the woman next to her start in surprise and shift away warily. She dug her phone out of her bag and was tempted to send him a shitty text to get in the last word but then thought—why bother? It was her own fault for thinking he could actually be a boyfriend. And that's what she wanted, she realised. There was no point trying to fit a square peg in a round hole, so to speak. She wanted a proper boyfriend, one that gave her a fully balanced nutritious meal of a relationship, not just the sex-on-the-side scraps. At least now she was free to find a guy she really liked. Life was too short to be with someone who couldn't appreciate *The Last of the Mohicans*.

Chapter 4

OLIVER

Oliver had decided to move closer to work, so he had found himself a flat within walking distance of his office in Farringdon. But he was starting to regret the decision to downsize his apartment. His room had shrunk in size accordingly, there being some sort of mathematical equation linking the distance from the centre of London to the exponential value of the size of an apartment. For the same price as a 50 sqm flat in Zone Four, Oliver was squished into a 30 sqm in Zone One. God knows what kind of shoebox you'd get if you actually lived right in Central London.

When Oliver had previously been fit, it was because he could roll out of bed and straight onto the treadmill. An hour later, he was dripping with sweat and able to jump into the shower. No possibility of not feeling like it, no excuses, no lying in bed doom-scrolling through social media. And afterwards? Energised, motivated, ready to take on the day.

Awesome! But now he didn't have enough space for a treadmill, and he didn't have a gym. There was no way in hell he was going to jog on the streets of London. Even if he got up really early there was something about breathing in exhaust fumes, slipping on black ice and dodging taxis, buses and cyclists that really didn't appeal. And there weren't any of London's green spaces nearby.

He briefly chuckled at the thought of trying to do reasonable kilometres by running around one of the little squares in Soho or Bloomsbury. You'd need to do a thousand laps to get a good run in and that would be more likely to make you dizzy than fit!

Of course, the gym that he had just left wasn't the only gym in town. Just the most insanely convenient. The next closest one was also convenient and featured a pool. But the monthly fees were almost as much as his rent. Sigh. He eventually found a new gym whose fees weren't too eye-watering and was within walkable distance. The walk did go past at least two chippies, three fried chicken shops and a gelateria, though. The gelateria was evidence that his neighbourhood was aiming for gentrification, which didn't really concern Oliver because he rented, but still might impact him with a rent increase at some point in the future. Still, worth a chortle seeing a poodle grooming salon sandwiched between the minicab office and the pound shop. Good luck to them!

The new gym, a twenty-minute walk away, was fine enough: a freshly painted building with motivational messages plastered on the walls in large silver metal letters. Feel the burn! Pain is weakness leaving the body! Push through it! Instead of those looking to maintain a certain body type, this one was more in line with Oliver's aspirations. Those who wanted to *change* their body type. Or those trying to hold off the ravages of old age.

Oliver had managed a week of regular attendance. And then a week of a little less regular attendance. Week three was sporadic. Week four, he went once.

That twenty-minute walk to get there was too much! Oliver breathed deeply. He could move further out into the suburbs and take the transport tax and waste hours fighting commuters to get in and out of London. But with the savings, he could go back to a treadmill beside his bed. Or find a gym with a pool and use his savings? Scratch that. He could ask for a raise at work and use that for the flash gym with the pool. Actually that would have to be a management role because the gym was just that expensive. And there was nothing to show that he was even next in line for a promotion when one came up.

So maybe he could just run to the gym? Use it as a warm-up? But that would involve running in London. One of the guys at work had done that. One of those two-percent-body-fat guys had boasted that he ran behind the buses on the road and only used the pavements to pass the buses when they stopped. Oliver hadn't seen him for a few weeks and had asked about him. Turns out that when buses stop to let people off, the departing passengers don't always look around as they get off and the runner had been clipped by a departing passenger and ended up flying head-first into a historically significant stone wall. The blood stain offset the blue plaque describing the historical significance very nicely.

He was chatting with Paul about it that night, lamenting his laziness.

'Oliver, you're giving yourself a hard time. Unnecessarily. You're creating a healthy habit. That's brilliant.'

'But I'm not going to the gym.'

'No, but you were. And you will again. But you have to figure out what it's going to take. Have you thought of getting a gym buddy? They're great to keep you honest. If someone is relying on you, then you're more likely to go.'

'Which gym do you use?'

'Sorry, I'm out in Zone Five. Anyone else at the gym you can buddy up with?'

Oliver thought about the others there. 'Maybe not so much.'

'Well, what about seeing a personal trainer a couple of

times a week? If you're lucky you can get one at a good rate.'

'A personal trainer?' Toby from work tried on the idea the next morning over coffee. 'Awesome, you can get some hot tight-body and check her out all session. It'll be like a private dancer. You'll have to get her to show you all the exercises,' he leered.

'I don't think so. I just want to get into the habit of going back to the gym. Get fit first and then out into the dating world.'

'Aw c'mon, man, everyone does that; they're used to it. They expect it. They like it, and even if she doesn't dig you, one of her hot gym friends will be gagging for it. Endorphins, innit? Like an aphrodisiac.'

Oliver looked at him. 'Really? It sounds really creepy. Like, so dodgy!'

'And if you're paying, then she has to do what you say.'

Oliver saw Toby in a new light. 'My God, you're a pervert! I thought you were just joking around, but you actually mean it!'

Toby looked defensive. 'Ah, no, not really. Just joking, just bants, man. Don't take it too seriously.'

Oliver shook his head. Nope, he wasn't going to be that guy. And just to make sure there's no chance of that happening, he would go out of his way to choose a male PT.

He couldn't be accused of leering at the PT if it was a guy. Well, you could if you were gay, but Oliver wasn't. And jeez, Toby, what a perve. He definitely didn't want to be mistaken as being in the same category as him.

Paul was more helpful. He had a list of recommendations on what he called his 'Page of Pain People', a list of all the personal trainers he'd used and their profiles.

'Why have you got so many? What's wrong with them? Surely you would just have one that you like?'

'Oh, I've moved a few times and I have one or two at each gym I've been to. Some are from word of mouth but I've never used. I keep them on the Page of Pain People because it's great to have someone I can get at the drop of a hat, no matter where I am. And they all have reasonable rates.'

'Awesome, thanks for that. I'll give one of them a go.'

Later on, Oliver went through the profiles. There were a couple that were in his neighbourhood and a few in the right price range. None of the profiles had pictures.

Derek: *Get results fast! We'll soon have you looking the way you want. I'm ex-Royal Marines and know how to motivate you to achieve your goals.*

More like dominate you, thought Oliver. That one sounded a lot like an hour of being yelled at.

George: *It starts now! It starts with you! I have 3% body fat and run marathons and I can get you taking minutes off your personal best. A targeted diet and training regime with supplements and concentrating on macro caloric deficit will guarantee results!*

Aw, man, that sounded like a whole lot of starving yourself! Oliver was starting to see a pattern emerging here.

Zee: *Do you like ice cream?*

What the? That was different. Um ... yes?

You can eat yummy food when you want, it's what you do most of the time that matters. I can help you develop healthy habits with treats and days off so that you keep coming back for more. Let's make exercise fun and focus on the process. The results will take care of themselves.

Winner! No yelling or starving or having a target, just putting the time in and making it a routine. He saw that Zee also had a BSc in Sport and Exercise Science and a Level 3 Personal Trainer qualification. Perfect! He texted the number on the list. Weird name though, 'Zee' must be short for Zebediah or some non-English name. Or maybe just some hipster thing. Maybe it was short for 'Zoltan'.

'Zoltan' responded pretty quickly, suggesting that they meet the next day at six at his gym for an assessment. The time suited, so he said yes and just like that he had a personal trainer.

The next day Oliver arrived at the gym on time, already changed and keen to get started. He looked around for Zoltan—he imagined him being of average height and either totally roided up or else one of those lean whippets who run a marathon before and after breakfast. He was loitering beside reception when one of the most beautiful women he'd ever seen came into the reception area. She was petite with blonde hair pulled back in a ponytail. She locked eyes with him, and he couldn't look away, the startling sapphires holding him like a laser tractor beam.

And then she actually walked right up to him and said something. He blinked and said, 'Hmm?'

'Are you Oliver? I'm Zee.'

Chapter 5

ZARA

By the time Zara reached her flat in Culmington Road, she was emotionally exhausted from thinking about why Jase had dumped her. All she wanted was to have a bath and go to bed. She went into the kitchen to deposit her empty lunch container in the dishwasher, but Erin was in there making hot chocolate. Her dark hair was scraped into a top-knot, and she was wearing her comfy watching-three-musicals-in-a-row attire: blue-and-white striped pyjama bottoms and a magenta long-sleeved t-shirt.

'Hey, you're home. I thought you were spending the night at Jase's?' she said.

'I was. But there was a change of plan. He dumped me.'

Erin's eyes widened. 'Oh shit. Sorry. Ouch. Are you OK?'

'Yeah, I guess so, thanks.' Zara sat down at the kitchen table, and Lala, who was underneath, started head-butting her shins, hoping for a snack. 'Hey, stop that!'

Erin took another cup down from the cupboard and nodded at the tin of hot chocolate. 'Want one?'

'Please.'

'So what happened? I thought you guys were really into each other.'

'Well, we weren't exactly the couple of the century, but we had some stuff in common and the sex was fantastic. Anyway, I just pushed for more and he didn't want it. Apparently even going to a movie was too much for him.'

'What did you see?'

'A rerun of *The Last of the Mohicans*. He laughed out loud when Alice jumped off the cliff.'

Erin looked flabbergasted. 'What the fuck?!'

Zara felt vindicated from her reaction. She didn't have to explain the importance of that scene, it was just intrinsic to someone who got it.

'I know! Then it came out that we don't have the same life philosophy apparently.' Her shoulders slumped.

'Honestly, Zee, he doesn't sound right for you at all. You deserve someone a lot better.' Erin handed her a cup of hot chocolate and patted her on the arm.

'Thanks for saying that.' They didn't usually do hugs, but Zara appreciated the moral support. Erin was the best. She was really fortunate to have her as a landlord.

They moved through into the lounge with their mugs, and

Zara saw Catherine Zeta-Jones paused on the TV screen with an arm flung out, her mouth twisted in a snarl. She looked to be part way through the line 'He had it coming …' Yikes! The last thing she felt like doing was watching *Chicago*! But luckily, Erin seemed content to keep talking rather than continue watching.

'Is it going to be awkward now, seeing him at the gym?' she asked, settling onto the couch with a packet of Jammie Dodgers.

Zara propped herself on the arm, ready to make a getaway if 'Cell Block Tango' came back on. 'Yup, I'm not looking forward to that.'

'Maybe you shouldn't shit where you eat from now on.'

'Huh?'

'I mean, steer clear of the PT guys at the gym. And just do online dating.'

Erin was probably right. But Zara couldn't see the point of going online. It was easier to date a PT guy since she was around them all the time and they were already interested in fitness. She just had to find one that had brawn *and* brains.

'It's more appropriate than going out with a client,' she huffed defensively. Clients did sometimes hit on her and ask her out, but she quickly gave them the usual spiel—*I'm flattered and thank you for asking, but it's not professional since you're a client.* So far, she hadn't actually been attracted to anyone who had asked her out. She wasn't sure what would happen if she was—it would definitely be hard to say no.

Her phone beeped with a text, and she checked the message.

'Is that Jase regretting his decision?' joked Erin.

'Nah, just someone wanting an assessment tomorrow after work.'

She quickly sent a text back to the guy: *Yes, I can see you at 6pm if that suits?*

He responded that it did, so she made a note in her Google calendar.

As she did so, she saw Erin's finger hovering over the play button on the remote, and Zara sensed that she was going to get roped into watching the rest of *Chicago* if she stayed in the lounge.

She downed the rest of her hot chocolate in one gulp. 'Right. I think I'll go to bed and leave you to it. Thanks for the hot chocolate and the chat. Oh and please don't let Lala have any of those Jammie Dodgers if she comes in. She's on a diet, remember?'

Erin nodded fervently. 'I won't.'

Later, when Zara was in bed, tossing and turning, trying to get to sleep, she hoped Jase *was* regretting his decision. But even if he tried to get her back, Zara didn't forgive and forget that easily. 'Onwards and upwards' was another one of her mottos.

Erin had already left for work when she got up the next morning. One of the great things about working on contract with the gym was that it was flexible hours. More often than not it meant a free morning because her clients tended to book training sessions during their lunch hours or after work. Today was one of those free morning days. Lala was in the kitchen and looking hopefully at her bowl. It was highly likely that Erin had already fed her, but Lala was an opportunist. If she saw a chance for a second breakfast, then she wasn't going to hesitate to take it.

'Hmm, have you already been fed?' Lala mewed and pawed her bowl, so Zara gave her the benefit of the doubt and some cat biscuits.

Her own breakfast consisted of wholegrain cereal with added flaxseeds, blueberries, banana and full-fat milk. She planned on exercising this morning and needed the protein.

Eating at the kitchen table, Zara contemplated her plan of action. A run in Walpole Park was definitely in order, it would help clear her head, and it was a nice day. Then maybe a yoga session for strength and balance. She could save her main workout for this afternoon at the gym in between clients. She had a few scheduled for today, starting with

Rebecca at 1pm and ending with the guy who'd contacted her last night, Oliver, at 6pm. Assessments were only half an hour, so she figured she'd be done by 6.30pm.

On the off-chance that her friend Amanda was free, Zara messaged to see if she wanted to go for a mocktail afterwards. Amanda was loved up with her fiancé Eli, but she was keen to go out if Eli was busy playing computer games. Although lately, she'd been busy with wedding arrangements since they were getting hitched in June. Zara had just begun warming up when Amanda messaged back, agreeing to the meetup.

Great idea! Eli's going to a concert with a friend, and I'm just mooching around here. Do you want to come over? We can have a girls' night and make our own drinks for free.

Zara raised her eyebrows. Funds were definitely tight! But Eli was going to a concert, so it seemed there was money in the kitty for him to enjoy himself? She didn't type her thoughts though. It was their business.

Sure sounds like fun. See you around 7pm. I'll come straight to yours after my last session.

Amanda and Eli lived in Shoreditch, an easy fifteen-minute walk from the gym. Sometimes Zara wished she wasn't so far out from the action. She liked living in West Ealing and the villagey feel of it but the gym, her friends and her mother were in Zone One. So that meant she was always travelling to them. Even Jase lived in Zone One. OK, he was flatting with three other guys, but at least he didn't have to ride the Tube for ages to get into work or see people.

Zara's stomach muscles tensed; there was a good chance she'd see him this afternoon since they both had clients on a Friday. She took a deep breath of morning air and did some lunges to get her blood pumping. Damned if she was going to let him see she was bothered by 'the dumping' as she'd started referring to it in her mind. She'd run him out of her system. If there was one thing she could count on, it was exercise. It never failed to put her in a good mood. And she needed to be chirpy and motivating for her clients. They weren't paying her to turn up sour-faced and moan about her personal problems. It was just a matter of keeping the facade in place for a few more hours and being Perfect Zara, the one that had everything together. She could break down and blub on Amanda's shoulder later. Though she didn't actually *feel* like breaking down or blubbing, it was good to know she could let her guard down if she needed to. They'd been friends since they were teenagers, and Amanda had been there for some of her best and worst moments. She supposed 'the dumping' counted as one of the latter.

In the late afternoon, Zara was sitting in the lunchroom eating grapes and cheese, scrolling on her phone and checking photos of Amanda and Eli's wedding venue. She'd seen it before, but she wanted it to be fresh in her mind in case Amanda freaked out over some detail. Fiona, Amanda's elder sister, was chief bridesmaid and had tasked her with the official job of 'calming the bride'.

'We don't want her stressing out and getting a face full of spots on her wedding day. There's only so much foundation can cover,' she'd cautioned at their planning session.

Thankfully, Fiona had taken on the lion's share of the organisation, as Zara had no clue where to even start. As one of the two minor bridesmaids, all she'd had to do so far was the fun stuff, like taste cake and offer her opinion on the wedding dress, flowers and the multitude of other minutiae that went into wedding preparation.

The wedding was in June, and Fiona had created a bridesmaids group on WhatsApp where she periodically counted down and freaked out when things went south, causing a flurry of supportive messages from the other bridesmaid, Melissa. Zara tried to stay out of the drama, stating that she didn't check her phone because she was usually working out with clients. So far she'd managed to fly under the radar. There had been an emphatic message this morning while she was on her run.

W-DAY IS OFFICIALLY FOUR MONTHS TODAY, PEEPS. JUST CONFIRMED FOR THE UMPTEENTH TIME THE CUTLERY IS TO BE SILVER NOT

CHROME. ARE THESE PEOPLE IDIOTS?!!

It sounded like Fiona was feeling the pressure, so Zara thought she better show that she *was* actually reading the messages and reacted with a sad face emoji.

Though now, as she gazed at the beautiful stately mansion deep in the Buckinghamshire countryside, complete with luxury rooms and rolling lawns, she realised that she was without a plus-one. She'd been planning to take Jase but hadn't asked him yet. But after last night and 'the dumping', there was no chance of that happening. Two of Eli's three groomsmen were Melissa's boyfriend and Fiona's husband, and she knew the other one had a girlfriend, so everyone was coupled up. The way things were looking, she'd be a wallflower when the dancing started.

One of the other PTs she was friendly with, Marsha, came in and sat down opposite her at the table, swilling from her water bottle.

'TGIF!' she said, smiling at Zara.

'Hear, hear,' she replied, and they bumped fists. 'How's things?'

Marsha sighed and released her tawny highlighted hair from her ponytail. 'Ergh. Just had the client from hell. She wants results and she wants it NOW. They don't seem to understand that this'—she waved a hand at her toned body—'has taken five years of discipline bordering on torture to achieve. It's not an overnight thing.'

Zara grinned. She'd had a similar experience with Rebecca just before. She was guzzling chocolate like it was going out of fashion and wondering why she still couldn't fit into her wedding dress. Zara was trying to be patient and keep her on track but it was difficult.

'I know the feeling,' she sympathised and offered Marsha her grapes.

They were munching and scrolling in companionable silence when Jase walked into the lunch room, closely followed by a female PT that had started the week before, Amber. Jase gave Zara and Marsha a polite nod, but that was it as far as acknowledgement went. He then proceeded to focus all his attention on Amber. Zara watched as they made protein shakes together and laughed over a shared private joke. *Wow*, she thought, taken aback. Jase had moved on faster than an alley cat with a hot tip about fresh fish.

Zara concentrated on her phone and tried not to look at them. Seriously? Did he have to flaunt his next conquest right in front of her? It was confirming her opinion that Jase was a monumental dickhead. Amber was welcome to him.

It was nearing 6pm, so Zara made an excuse to Marsha about meeting her next client and, blatantly ignoring Jase and the giggling, blushing Amber, went out to reception to meet Oliver. This was good, it was a clean break. If he could move on, then so could she. Zara took a deep breath and tried to emanate positive vibes. A tall, well-padded guy with brown hair and a gym bag was hanging around the reception area, looking at some pamphlets. She took a chance that this was him, so she introduced herself, but he didn't seem to hear, just looked at her and said, 'Hmm?'

Maybe he was a bit deaf? She repeated herself and enunciated clearly so he could see her lips. 'Are you Oliver? I'm Zee.'

Chapter 6

OLIVER

With Toby's words about objectifying his female PT resounding in his ears, Oliver made a concerted effort to listen to the words Zee was saying and to ignore what she looked like. This was difficult.

'First of all, what are your goals? What do you want to achieve?' she asked.

The ceiling: look at the ceiling. 'Well, I'm very unfit. But I used to be ... fit, I mean. Not like "fit fit", but I used to be able to climb the stairs at work without puffing, so I'd like to go back to that.'

'And that's all?'

'Yeah, pretty much.'

'Well, that's a relief. I can't tell you how many men I get who want to look like Brad Pitt from *Fight Club*.'

'Look, if I focus on the fitness element, then I figure that will lead to the belly going and a bit of muscle tone.'

'Very sensible! OK, that sounds great. We'll get you to do a food diary of everything you eat during the week.'

Oliver's face dropped. 'You said in your profile that I'd be able to have my ice cream?'

He mentally kicked himself. He sounded like a child!

She smiled reassuringly. 'Oh, you can! I do too. I'm a sucker for a Magnum. We just need to baseline your calorific inputs so we can achieve a deficit. We want calories out to be greater than calories in. And your fitness and muscle power are the engine which drives it.'

She glanced at his chest for emphasis when she talked about muscle power, and Oliver felt a little flutter. Zee *looked* exactly like the sort of girl that Oliver wanted to go out with. But what about her personality? Maybe she was a bitch? And even if she wasn't, Oliver was paying her to be with him, so she was off-limits. But he very desperately wanted her to like him. So he had to ace this assessment.

'Shall we see how well you do on the bike?' Zee asked, leading the way to the exercycles.

'Sure,' he agreed, clambering awkwardly onto the bike.

'So let's start off at a four difficulty and see how long you can go for.'

'OK,' Oliver said and started pedalling. It was quite hard work, and two minutes later, he had a nice sweat going. Five minutes in he started to run out of puff and after eight minutes he had to stop.

'Great work,' said Zee as she made a few notes.

'I ... I ... could have ... gone a little ... bit longer,' managed Oliver.

'Of course.' Zee grinned. 'How about you catch your breath, and then we'll see how you go on the weight machines.'

Oliver barely suppressed his panic.

'Um, I was thinking we could just work on cardio for my fitness,' he managed.

'Sure, we'll definitely do that, but we need to also look at developing your muscles so that they can support the levels of activity that you want to do. If you only do cardio, eventually you'll push your legs to do something which your back muscles won't be able to support. And then you'll pull a muscle or injure yourself. And your back muscles can't be out of alignment with your shoulders and your chest, and then your arms and neck will be out of whack—it's all a connected system.'

'Ah, OK then.' Oliver guessed he would be on the weight machines quite a bit then.

'First up, just a basic bench press. How much should we try?'

'I don't know, fifty kilos?'

Zee's eyes narrowed. 'Hmm, maybe not to start with.

How about you try fifteen—that's five plus the bar?'

She showed him how to put the weights on the machine and how to position his body.

He pushed. And pushed. OMG this was hard. Eventually he got the thing off his chest and struggled with wobbly arms to raise the bar to the full extent. He lowered it rather quickly, and the bar returned to its cradle with more of a crash than he expected.

'Cool, let's grab a drink of water,' said Zee, making another note as they walked over to the water station. She put the open notebook down as she took a sip, and Oliver, to avoid looking at her leggings-clad butt, glanced at it. It had originally had *Bench: 8 reps of* _____ *kg* written on it but that had been crossed out and replaced with *Bench: 1 rep of 15 kg*, so he had the feeling that he was underwhelming her. This was him at his worst, in a field he was terrible at, and he was trying to make a good first impression. He was dying here.

'You mentioned that you lived in Farringdon? I couldn't figure out why you would be coming to this gym. Surely you have to pass at least two other gyms before reaching this one? I mean, I don't mind, I can meet you at any of them, but ...?'

'Well, you know the one on Garrett Street, that's like megabucks, so I can't afford that one.'

'And the one on Banner Street?'

'Well ... let's just say that I did go to that one for a while.'

'And ...?'

'There were one or two ... things that happened ... that I'm not incredibly proud of. If we go ahead long term, maybe I'll tell you about them.'

She looked at him sharply. 'Nothing inappropriate, I hope?'

'Oh, no, nothing like that. Perfectly innocuous!' And then to avoid further scrutiny, he said, 'So, what's next?'

'Shall we try legs?'

'Sure!'

Mindful of the fact that she expected him to do multiple exercises for the assessment, he set the weight to the first setting, hoping that he'd be able to do a lot of a smaller weight rather than expending all his energy in one go.

The first down and up was good, as was the second. The third started to get a little hard, and then the fourth was a bit of an effort. Five and six were like pulling teeth, and he really had to push hard on number seven. Huffing and puffing and groaning with effort, he finally got number eight done before slumping on the floor beneath the machine.

'Well done, great effort.' Zee beamed as he tried to look nonchalant. From the floor.

'I could probably do another two sets of those,' he told her between pants, trying for a modest tone.

'Oh, that's probably enough for the assessment; we'll

work up to that in our sessions.'

Thank God, he thought as he heaved himself off the floor.

'Can I get you to jump up on the scales?'

Oh dear, Oliver thought. *This is not going to be good.* Zara noticed his hesitation.

'It's purely to set a benchmark. None of the goals you've talked about are weight related, so we're just going to write down the number and then ignore it. Sorry, we won't ignore it, we'll weigh you every month or six weeks just to make sure things aren't getting out of hand. We have to make sure that any progress is maintainable. No point in starving yourself to get the magic number moving and then put it all back on when you start eating again, right?'

Oliver stepped up on the scales and watched as the digital numbers slowly settled. 'I'm also wearing my trainers, which are probably quite heavy,' he said, willing the numbers to lower themselves magically. 'And don't forget muscle is heavier than fat.'

Zara smiled at him. 'I'll add a note to that effect,' she said as she wrote in her notebook. 'I'll send you a link for the food diary. Just a few pointers: make sure that you put everything that you eat in the diary, and if you have anything special, make a mark to show that it's a once-a-week or once-a-month type treat, and we can get a feel of what your normal diet looks like. And that's it: assessment over! That wasn't too bad now, was it?'

Oliver smiled back. Only time would tell.

An hour later he was back at his flat, freshly showered, chatting online with his best friend Mark. He'd met Mark while he was a first year living on campus at UCL. They'd both come from small towns in the Midlands and together they had negotiated the big city lights. After they had graduated, they still kept in touch even though Oliver had stayed in London and Mark had gotten jobs in New York, Chicago and now in Dubai. Oliver knew Mark did something involving the defence industry, which required a high security clearance, but he also knew that he couldn't say much about it. There was usually plenty to chat about though, even if they couldn't talk about work. Lately, that involved talking over the internet while Mark played some sort of shoot 'em up online and Oliver played something more sedate.

'So you're going to the gym, that's good. *Eat shit, you camper!*'

'Yeah, Zee is a hottie and a half. Super hot, super nice.'

'Zee? So you've got a female trainer?'

'Yeah, I didn't want one but that's just how it panned out.'

'Great, great! *Cover me, you assholes. Point your guns that way. Not this way. That way! Now spray them. Muppets!* Any chance of romance there, buddy?'

'I don't think so, I'm not exactly in shape, remember?'

'Yeah, but—*hey, butt munch, move it, you're supposed to be in my squad, so move it!* Sorry, where was I? Yeah, don't underestimate your winning personality. Spend a little time with her, and who knows where it will end?'

'That would kind of feel a little weird. I'm paying her for three sessions a week. If I start telling her jokes and stuff, she will just be laughing because I'm paying her. I don't need to pay for pity laughs; I get enough of those already!'

'Well, if your material was any better, you wouldn't have those issues—*Defuse the bomb. I'll cover you. Sorry, I didn't see that guy there. Oh shut up; you'll respawn soon enough. Jerk.*'

'Seriously, you like that game? The people always seem so toxic.'

'What, you think that giving people an anonymous platform and then running the adrenaline up with a life-and-death scenario would somehow put a bunch of immature man-babies under more stress than they can handle? Do me a favour ... and I'm dead. Snipers, man. Look, the round restarts in thirty seconds, so listen up. You've started a journey which is great. You've taken control of the situation, and as long as you stick with it, you've got a really good chance of getting the results that you want. I'm proud of you, man. It's the first step on the road to getting yourself out there. But just don't let perfection get in the way of good. That means even if you're working on being a better version of yourself, don't forget that you've got a whole lot to offer now. You're a great guy, and you deserve every bit of happiness. So don't sell yourself short.'

'Thanks, Mark. I appreciate it.'

'*Drop dead, you mungo mother fucker!* Sorry, spawn camper got me as soon as I spawned. I hate that.'

Chapter 7

ZARA

Being her last client of the day, Oliver was front of mind when Zara was heading to Amanda's. His assessment had been one of the more interesting ones. Despite being woefully out of shape, he obviously had motivation and hadn't baulked when she'd run through a suggested training programme. They were going to be working out three times a week, and she was looking forward to helping him achieve his fitness goals. She was impressed that he wanted to get fit purely under his own steam, not because his girlfriend was nagging him or he had an upcoming wedding. Zara tried to visualise what he would look like ripped but couldn't quite picture it. Anyway, building muscles wasn't something Oliver had seemed overly concerned about. He was more focused on the health side of things. She wondered what had happened at the other gym to get him kicked out and hoped he wasn't going to be a Rebecca about the ice cream.

Spring was making an appearance in this corner of East London. As Zara walked down the street, she could see buds on the brown spindly branches of trees and there was a tang of freshness in the air. The lighter evenings were also a relief after the cold dark months of winter. Amanda and Eli lived in a 1930s-style red brick apartment block with a curved wraparound balcony. As it came into view, Zara instinctively glanced up at the second storey. Amanda was out there waiting for her, and she waved and called down. 'Hellloooo. I'm getting married in four months! And the cutlery has only just been sorted. Arrgggh!' She clawed at her face dramatically and Zara laughed. Fiona's message had obviously made it out of the WhatsApp group and found its way to the bride. Or she'd forwarded it to her to show her exactly what she was having to put up with. Either way, Zara was glad Amanda wasn't taking the whole thing too seriously.

Inside, she found her friend preparing her version of pineapple daiquiris—fruit juice, a tin of pineapple, Sprite, ice, and coconut cream were displayed on the kitchen counter. The ingredients had been placed in a blender and the contents of a large bottle of vodka was currently being poured in.

'Hey, I said *mocktails*. Easy on the vodka,' protested Zara.

Amanda snorted. 'You PTs are so bloody healthy. You never treat yourself.'

'I'm not that healthy,' said Zara, hanging her jacket on the back of a nearby chair. 'Last night I had a Magnum, popcorn *and* a hot chocolate.'

'That's not like you. How come?'

The mix was whizzed on high for thirty seconds at an ear-splitting roar (the blender was not a high-end model), and when it was quiet again, Zara replied, 'I was out with Jase. We went to a movie.'

Amanda handed her a tall yellow cocktail, complete with a tiny colourful umbrella.

'Oh wow. You two are really progressing. Let's go into the lounge.' The flat had been renovated as open plan, and the lounge was a separate area with a three-seater couch, an easy chair, a glass coffee table and assorted house plants.

Seating herself in the chair and leaving the couch for Amanda, Zara debated whether she should mention 'the dumping'. It could add to the bride's stress quotient if she knew she was without a plus-one. But she needed to vent. And the wedding was still a few months away, surely she could find someone else in that time?

'Ah, actually we're not. He dumped me. Unceremoniously. Outside the Barbican Cinema.'

Amanda's eyes widened. 'What?'

Zara shrugged. 'It's no biggie. He was on the way out anyway.'

'But weren't you going to take him to our—' Amanda started with a frown, and Zara cut her off at the pass.

'Your wedding is ages away. I'll find a plus-one easily before then.'

'I'm not worried,' Amanda said, pushing the umbrella aside and taking a long sip of her cocktail. 'You have your pick of men. You could ask a guy on the street and he'd go with you.'

'I don't think so,' Zara scoffed. 'Why do I even need someone anyway? I'm a bridesmaid, I'm going to be sitting at the top table at the reception. I won't even be with them for the dinner.'

'I know, it's just for *afterwards*. For the dancing and downtime, someone to cosy up with. I don't want you stuck with Uncle John; believe me, that isn't an experience I'd wish on anyone.'

Zara sighed. 'Fine. I'll do my best.'

'You must have someone you can take from the gym apart from Jase. Are you training anyone nice?'

Oliver flashed into Zara's mind. He was tall, seemed intelligent and was attractive.

'Yes, but he's a client, so he's off-limits.'

'Can't you make an exception?'

Zara hesitated. Clients were her bread and butter. She couldn't take the risk. What if it all went horribly wrong?

No—clients were definitely off-limits.

'Nope,' she said firmly. 'As Erin says, I shouldn't shit where I eat. She has a point.'

Amanda raised an eyebrow. 'And Erin's such an expert on men. Is she still sitting home alone and watching musicals?'

Zara nodded, feeling a bit bad for Erin. She shouldn't have brought her up. She and Amanda didn't get on too well. Not for any particular reason, just a personality clash. Erin could be a bit of a know-it-all, and Amanda found it irritating, which was why Zara didn't invite her over to the flat too often. She changed the subject hurriedly.

'So how's the wedding prep going?'

'It's going. Fi has everything under control by the sounds of it.'

'What's left to do?'

'The seating arrangements at the reception and your bridesmaid dresses. She's probably going to need your help with that one.'

'Why?' Zara tried to sound curious and not defensive.

'Because you're the only one who's seen my wedding dress. And the bridesmaid dresses have to follow along the same theme but not steal my thunder. "No bride wants her bridesmaids looking hotter than her on her big day"—Fi's words.'

Zara pulled a face, and Amanda giggled. 'I still can't

believe neither of them could make the wedding dress appointment. Fiona must've been gutted,' she said.

'I think it was definitely one of her low points,' Amanda replied. 'But they didn't tell me the date wasn't good for them, so how was I supposed to know? I don't have kids so why would I keep track of these things?'

Fiona and Melissa both had a couple of kids each and the wedding dress appointment had been the first day of the Spring school holidays. A fact that they hadn't realised until the Sunday night a week before and by then it was too late to change the appointment. They'd bowed out to oversee playdates or outings, so it had been just her and Amanda. Zara had lounged around on a pink felt couch, sipped champagne and nibbled on dark chocolate almonds, while Amanda had flounced in and out of the room in different white creations. It had been a fun morning, especially when Amanda had come out in an off-the-shoulder satin dress, stared at herself in the mirror, and they'd exclaimed in sync: 'Oh my God. That's the one!'

'To be honest, I don't really care what you guys wear,' said Amanda, stabbing at a piece of floating pineapple with her cocktail stick. 'Just for the love of God, don't let Fiona choose purple. She loves it but I hate that colour. It's so old-fashioned too. And no one looks good in it. Except maybe Scarlett Johansson.'

Zara laughed. 'OK. No purple!'

'And the hen do is coming along.' Fiona had been organising that as well.

'Oh yeah, anything good? There's probably not going to be a stripper, is there?'

Amanda shook her head and laughed. 'Definitely not. She's thinking of a terrarium class.'

'A what?' Zara asked, confused.

'You know, creating a garden in a jar?'

Zara snorted. 'For a hen do? That sounds as fun as a root canal.'

'She said it would be suitable for a range of people.'

Zara pressed her lips together, trying not to laugh at Amanda's blank expression. 'Which people exactly? Not us! Don't you have a say? You are the hen!'

'I don't want to step on her toes. You know what she's like.' Zara didn't really but she was beginning to. She unlocked her phone and googled 'hen do ideas London'.

'Look at this—we can float around in a hot tub in the Thames and have some drinks and food; that looks fun. You can even keep the sailor hat. Or what about a walking silent disco?'

'Those do sound like something I'd enjoy more,' Amanda agreed. 'I'll give her your suggestions.'

Zara crossed her fingers but wasn't hopeful.

Chapter 8

OLIVER

Ouch, ouch, ouch, ouch.

Everything hurt. He'd totally wrecked himself in a session two days ago, and now it was painful to do anything strenuous. Three weeks in and he was still trying to impress Zee, and he didn't think that was having any effect at all. Oliver finally figured out that Zee would have seen and had clients who would be proper athletes, so there was no way that she would be impressed by the 'before' in his 'before and after' journey. She was never dismissive and had been really encouraging, but then again, that was her job. He shook his head. Even the non-physical stuff hadn't gone well.

'So, what do you do?' she'd asked as he rested between sets of bench presses.

'I work in a call centre,' he answered, wincing internally. Nobody ever understood his job.

'What, like answering calls?'

'Not exactly. I program IVRs.'

'IVRs?'

'Interactive voice responses. You know when you ring up some big company and the system says something like (he switched to an exaggerated professional voice) "Press 1 for accounts. Press 2 for sales"? Yeah, well, I program those responses and the routes that you go through before you speak to someone.'

'I thought that happened automatically.'

'Oh, no. Someone has to program those. And then tweak them based on what is working and what isn't working. Like if you have too many internal transfers, that might be a sign that you haven't made the menu selection clear enough.'

'But surely that doesn't change enough to warrant a full-time position?'

OK, great, so she understood the actual job, but she just didn't think that it was enough of a career. 'Well, you also have a look at the numbers that people use to ring in and where they're getting those numbers. Plus how many are choosing which routes and whether that is the most efficient. There's a lot of scope there for making changes.'

'OK, well, it's obviously working out for you. What else do you like doing?'

'I love travelling! Last month, I went to Jordan. Petra was amazing. And this time I also went to Wadi Rum, where they filmed *Dune* and *The Martian*.'

'Yeah, I've got a list of places where I want to go. I haven't started yet, but one day. Maybe when I've got lots of clients,' she said with a grin.

Oliver bit his lip. 'Yeah, but then you will have so many clients that you won't be able to go; otherwise, who'll be there to make sure your clients go to the gym?'

'Good point,' she replied. Almost as if to change the subject, she continued, 'I'll probably have to get a passport, though.'

'You don't have a passport?'

'Well, I had one when I went to France in school, but with one thing and another, I haven't quite gotten around to heading back overseas. So I didn't renew it. I'm pretty sure I don't look anything like that photo now. I've been meaning to get one for a while now; the renewals don't take long.'

The conversation seemed to be petering out, and Oliver was worried that they would move onto one of the weight machines. 'So, is the personal training thing the end goal? Is that what you always wanted to do?'

She seemed surprised by the question and instantly brightened. 'I love being a trainer. I can help people reach their goals, and I get fit doing it. It's brilliant! I have total flexibility in my schedule, so I'm not stuck in a nine-to-five, and as long as I get as many new clients as the number that drop off, I can pay my bills. It's a great life.' She looked at him sharply but with a grin. 'I think you're stalling, though. Shall we do some press-ups?'

Oliver's office was one of those exposed brick jobs with open plan hot desking and open ceilings, the kind where the wires snaking across the ceilings were a feature rather than evidence that the indoor decorating was unfinished and/or dangerous. But the most annoying thing was the lift.

'Lift out again?'

'Yup.'

And so it was up the stairs. The lift went out of commission every other month, and when it did, if you were stuck inside, then say goodbye to your day. The only way to get you out was to call an engineer and they took their merry time in attending. And then it was another couple of weeks' wait for the part to make it work again.

So the staircase got a lot of action. Although Oliver wasn't fit, he could go up the stairs in one direction without getting puffed. And then he usually had a rest at his desk. And if there was a meeting on a different floor, he could get there without embarrassing himself. The only time the lack of fitness showed was when he had to do two trips on the stairs one after another.

Like his 10am meeting, waiting on the boss to go through the company-wide announcements. Samara and Toby were shooting the shit while they waited. Well, the other two did while Oliver tried to catch his breath.

He saw them share a glance and held up a finger. 'I'm ... fine ... just ... give me ... a ... minute.'

'It's quite the long climb up those stairs,' commiserated Samara, who went by the nickname Sam. She was loved up, recently married even though she was in her early twenties, just out of university. Her family were originally from India but had been in England for three generations. Enough time to take on the accent of her private schools and avoid an arranged marriage. But not too long to forget how to make jalebis and do traditional dances at weddings while wearing a sari.

'Yeah, we should probably move the meeting to a room on our floor,' Toby added. 'We tried last month, but the design team needed the extra space. I don't know why, though. Are they still discussing the relative merits of different shades of blue? Anyways, did you have a good weekend, Oliver? Meet any nice ladies?'

Oliver shook his head. 'No, I want to lose this weight before I get into online dating.' He indicated his belly with a frown.

Toby, who was never short of an opinion, had some thoughts on the subject of his gym attendance. He was a similar shape to Oliver but without the height and an ...

interesting approach to personal hygiene. His beard was patchy and somehow the patches always seemed to be in different spots from week to week. Truly bizarre, and Oliver had never quite figured that out.

'I actually don't think that you need to attend the gym to find someone,' he stated.

'Oh?'

'Nope, what you need is a chick with a crush fetish.'

Oliver looked blankly at Sam, who shook her head. 'What do you mean?'

'I'm glad you asked.' Toby settled into his chair. 'It's come to my attention from my online journeys that there is a huge range of sexual preferences. If you pull the nation's bedcovers back, the shenanigans that people get up to would boggle your mind, and it's all sorts doing it too. Professionals, manual labourers, office workers, the lot. Anyways, I went down a rabbit hole the other day and found something interesting: people that like being crushed. Some guys and some girls like the physical sensation of being squeezed. There's also fan art in their communities of giant boa constrictors which are some truly disturbing images, but in the forums, they talk about wanting to be with someone who can "push the air out of their lungs" that sort of thing.'

Oliver didn't know what to say, so said nothing. Sam looked fascinated but whether it was with the subject matter or the way Toby was talking about it in the office, he wasn't sure.

'So I think you shouldn't be trying to make yourself smaller. Nope, you should be finding someone who can love you for who you are,' he said triumphantly, as if he had laid out a convincing legal argument in front of a judge.

Oliver blinked.

Sam was all intense and well-meaning. 'It shouldn't matter what you look like, Oliver. You just be yourself. If it's meant to be, it will be. People should see your personality; they should look beyond the superficial.'

Toby grinned with barely contained glee. 'So what you're saying, Sam, is that he's such a Quasimodo that the girls should just put up with that?'

Realising what she'd said, Sam tried backpedalling. 'Oh, no, I didn't mean …'

'That's fine, Sam. I think I know what you were trying to say. And it would be lovely if that was the case. But don't I deserve to have someone who is wildly nuts over what I look like and wants to make manic love to me because of how hot I look? That we have that layer of lust in the relationship as well as a deep emotional connection?'

'"Layer of Lust"? Sounds like Chicken Porn,' said Toby.

'You know what I mean,' Oliver continued. 'Like when you go on a site, you obviously swipe through looking for the hotties. You don't read the profiles and think, "Hey, that's a nice person".'

'You do need that spark,' agreed Sam. 'Like with me and Darren. The minute he walked into the halls of residence, I knew he was the one for me.'

Toby shook his head. 'Yeah, but you can get that spark from talking to someone too. In fact, that instant attraction thing is just a reaction to how good-looking they are. That spark, though, that's when you're vibing with someone, and you get where they're coming from, but they still surprise you.'

Oliver was surprised at something insightful coming out of Toby's mouth that wasn't offensive, immoral or illegal. Or all three. 'You might be onto something there, Toby,' he said.

Chapter 9

ZARA

The weeks flew by, and the wedding date loomed ever closer, but Zara was still no further to finding a plus-one. She'd almost resigned herself to the fact that she was attending the wedding alone. It was no big deal. There was just the ceremony to get through. And the reception afterwards. OK, and the buffet breakfast for friends and family the next morning. Damn, Amanda was right. She was going to get stuck with Uncle John if she didn't find someone to take, and soon. Maybe Melissa had a brother or a cousin? She made a mental note to send a separate WhatsApp message to her. The worst she could do was tell Fiona, and they'd giggle and talk about her behind her back for being no-date Nancy.

Zara heaved a sigh as she stepped off the Tube at Euston. It was Saturday morning, and she was visiting her mum, Kate, who lived in a Victorian brick apartment building in Tavistock Place. Her living situation was similar to Zara's.

She was renting with another lady in her sixties called June, but in this case, June didn't own the flat. An unseen male landlord, Mr Davies, did.

Kate and June had never met him, they just paid the rent dutifully each week into his account. He'd never increased the rent once since they'd been living there, and that was getting on for ten years. So in that respect, he was a good landlord. But Zara thought it was weird he never replied to any messages about repairs or indeed any messages at all to do with the flat—the women just sorted any issues themselves and split the bill.

Zara didn't like to think it but perhaps he'd died years ago and no one knew? His bank account would just keep growing bigger and bigger with all their rent money. She was pretty sure she was being silly and Mr Davies wasn't dead, but it was slightly strange. She'd mentioned it to her mum once, but she'd laughed and said Mr Davies was just a very private person, and if there was a real emergency, he'd reply to their messages. And that people didn't die without anyone knowing. Someone would miss him. Especially if he owned real estate. But Zara wasn't so sure. There were plenty of odd bods in London who lived alone and had no family.

Thinking of odd bods who lived alone, Oliver's face flashed into her mind before she could help it. After a few months of working out with him, she'd learned enough to know he wasn't a weirdo; he was a nice guy—but still, he was just a bit … different from other guys she knew.

Zara walked past the local shop where her mum worked during the week selling natural health and wellness products. She also tinkered around at home, making her own, though not very successfully. Her last batch of herbal-infused moisturiser had given Zara, who had been the guinea pig, a nasty leg rash. Those ones had been hastily binned. Kate was also into holistic healing rituals, including crystals, reiki, acupuncture and massage and had a number of regular local clients. Not able to afford the lease on a studio, she was using the flat lounge for her home business. She'd even had a stack of business cards made up to hand out on the sly in the shop. When Zara saw them, she'd been confused. *STORM STEVENS* was printed on the card with the symbol of a pair of hands, along with an email address of the same name and Instagram handle.

'Who's Storm Stevens?'

'Me, dear.'

'But why not just use your real name?'

'Kate is boring. "Storm Stevens" has such a wonderful ring to it, don't you think? Almost like I could be a member of Fleetwood Mac.'

Zara had cracked up. Her mother was a hoot at the best of times, but this really tickled her. She had to admit she was enterprising.

'I guess it's a good thing Mr Davies doesn't do regular flat inspections then. He might not appreciate his flat being used as a health and wellness clinic. What does June think about all this?'

'She's fine about it.'

'Really? You've taken over the lounge.'

Kate had averted her eyes. 'Well, I had to bribe her with a free massage twice a month, but she hardly ever uses it anyway. She's always over at Gordon's.'

Gordon was June's latest boyfriend she'd met on an internet dating site, and they'd been seeing each other for six months, a record according to Kate. This was part of the reason why Zara was visiting today. She was wanting to catch up with her mum but also keen to pick June's brains for tips about how she'd managed to nab a nice guy on an internet dating site.

The first words out of Kate's mouth when she'd finished hugging Zara were, 'You feel tense. Let me give you an acupuncture session.' She poked a finger into her shoulder muscle, and Zara brushed her hand away.

'I'm fine, Mum. I don't need acupuncture.' She shuddered, that was something else she'd been the guinea pig for, and she'd ended up looking like a voodoo doll. 'I'm just a bit stressed. Is June here?'

Kate led the way into the kitchen and flicked the kettle on. 'No, she's not. She and Gordon have gone away for the weekend ... to stay in an Airbnb in Wales,' she added in case Zara needed more details. 'Why?'

Zara sat down at the kitchen table, feeling even more stressed. 'Amanda's wedding is coming up fast, and I need to find a plus-one. I thought she could give me some internet dating tips.'

Kate rummaged through myriad boxes of herbal tea on the kitchen counter before finding what she was looking for. 'Ah yes, lavender mint, good for stress. So what happened to Jason?'

'He dumped me,' said Zara flatly, not really wanting to get into it.

'Oh no. Why? He seemed so nice.'

'I don't know why you'd think that. You never even met him,' said Zara. Kate had only seen the sneaky photo of him working out at the gym that she'd taken.

'Well, he looked like a lovely boy; he had very nice biceps.'

'He wasn't. He only thought about himself. Now he's with Amber. I don't care.'

'Sounds like you do care a bit,' said Kate gently, handing her a cup of tea and sitting down opposite her. 'Why do you need someone for the wedding anyway? It's not going to be a coupley affair, is it? You don't need a man to have a good time.'

'You don't need a man to have a good time' was Kate's catchphrase, and one she trotted out any chance she could. Zara's father, Jack, had died from a heart attack when he was in his early fifties due to his liking for pies and pints. The local pub had been his second home. His death was the reason that Zara, who had just turned twenty at the time, decided to become a personal trainer and why her mother was now a stickler about health and wellness. Zara knew her mum had sworn off men, but what was so wrong with being loved up and eventually settling down? It sounded pretty good to her. Turning up alone to Amanda's wedding would just reinforce everything she wanted but didn't have. It would be a singleton's nightmare.

She sipped her lavender mint tea and sighed. 'You know what weddings are like. I'll get lumped with all the other single people, like Amanda's Uncle John.'

'What's wrong with Uncle John?'

'He's a perpetual bachelor, an eccentric. He'll trap me and insist on talking about his trains all night.'

Kate's lips twitched. 'He doesn't sound too bad.'

'Mum!'

'If you really need someone to go with you, I could help.'

'How?'

'I'll keep an eye out at the shop during the week. We get a

lot of young men coming in to buy herbal deodorant and vitamins.'

Zara sniggered. 'So you're just going to say, "My daughter needs a plus-one for her friend's wedding, do you want to go with her?"'

'Something along those lines, yes. Don't worry, I'll make sure they're not buying herbal Viagra or anything like that first.'

'Oh God. I can't believe I'm agreeing to this, but OK.' Zara shook her head. What new level of desperateness had she just stooped to?

Chapter 10

OLIVER

Oliver didn't know if he hated the treadmill or the weights more. The treadmill was a solid block of time where he was sweaty and disgusting and the number on the LED readout for speed was nowhere near representing the amount of effort that he was expending. Whenever he looked despondent, Zara would give him a reminder of a little speech she'd given him when they'd started.

'Look, you're starting from scratch, so give yourself a break. We want to get you so that you're running at eight kilometres per hour for a full thirty minutes. But that won't happen straight away. So here's what we'll do. Have two minutes of warm-up just walking, whatever speed you can do. And then crank it up to how fast you can run. Doesn't matter if it's not eight but push yourself. You'll run out of puff pretty quickly to start with, and then—this is the important bit—lower it by half a kilometre per hour and walk really fast. More of a march. And keep doing that as long as you can. And if you get your breath back, bump it back up and see how long you can run again. The goal is to keep your average speed as high as possible until you get that fitness so that you can maintain a full half-hour at the higher speed.'

'Why not just go straight for eight?'

'Your body can't handle that. We need to build up your muscles so that you can support moving your body consistently and then move on to the speed. We're aiming to get your heart rate in the right zone.'

It was good that he didn't feel like he was failing when he couldn't run any further, just pushing his body's abilities. The other good thing was that Zara was on the treadmill beside him. When he reached the point where he couldn't keep running and bumped the speed down a few notches, he glanced over to see if Zara had noticed, and she met his eye and gave him a thumbs-up. She was jogging lightly herself and moving very smoothly, ponytail swishing from side to side. He was surprised that her LED read eight kph as she didn't seem bothered by the speed. It was comforting that she was there beside him. He didn't feel like he was alone in his efforts, even if he was definitely doing all the work!

His speed lowered; he maintained an uncomfortably fast march for the rest of the session, sweating profusely by the end of it. When the thirty minutes clicked over, and the machine gradually stopped, he hung onto the rails and looked over at Zara for the verdict.

'Great work!' she said, and it sounded like she meant it. 'You kept your average speed up which was awesome!'

He felt like shit.

'I feel like shit,' he told her between pants.

'You will for a period. You're shocking your body out of complacency, and that will have an effect. Your body will complain for a while. It's important to keep the rhythm going. So ... you mentioned at your assessment that you had a few reasons why you changed gyms?'

Oliver was torn. On one hand, he wanted to keep resting and let his muscles recover from the treadmill. On the other hand, he really didn't want to tell any of his stories. They definitely didn't paint him in the best light. But he had said. Maybe just the most innocent story.

'So ... I had a metal drink bottle. You know those aluminium ones with the complicated sippers?'

Zara nodded.

'Well, I was on the treadmill at the other gym with my water bottle and was listening to music on my phone and went to skip a song. They didn't have the holder for them like we do here, and so the phone moved a bit as I was running, and it looked like it was going to fall off the treadmill. I lunged for it and knocked my water bottle off the holder; it landed on the treadmill, which launched it across the room. You know that the gym has their stretching area just behind the cardio machines?' Zara nodded again.

'So some poor person sitting on the mat doing stretches got my metal water bottle launched at their head at a hundred miles an hour. OK, maybe only a few miles per hour. But, man, that made a huge sound as it hit the concrete wall behind them. Everyone turned to see what was going on, such a big bang sounded like a gong. I was lucky it missed, but there was a report and a talk, and they made a little note on my record.' He looked over to see if she was judging him harshly. She was smiling good-naturedly, which he interpreted as a good thing.

Six weeks after starting, they debriefed on his dietary diary.

'Great news, Oliver. You're eating healthily with a good combination of proteins and fats and carbohydrates. It won't be hard to get into caloric deficit by increasing the amount of exercise you're getting so the side effect of you getting fitter will naturally be that you will lose weight. As I said last time, we'll only weigh you periodically because as you get more and more exercise you will convert the fat into muscle. That's going to weigh more, and so if we focus on your weight, we'll be getting the wrong message. Hey, I've even had clients gain weight because they were fixated on the numbers on the scales, and then, of course, they became quite despondent. We don't want that to happen! Monitoring your weight is more to make sure we pick up on any unsustainable weight loss.'

Oliver let out a breath he hadn't realised he'd been holding. 'That's great! Really is ... um ... and as for the ice cream?'

Zara smiled. 'Hey, what's important is what you eat every day, day in, day out. If you have a blowout day every fortnight or every month, that's fine. And you're allowed a treat every now and again as well. So definitely have your ice cream. It's great that you only have takeaways twice a week, and one of those is sushi, so it's not problematic from a saturated fat point of view. So keep doing what you're doing. One of the meals you mention is interesting: tell me about your rice, veg and salmon?'

'Oh, that's one of those two-minute sachets of microwave rice, a boil-in-the-bag thing of vegetables and a pre-cooked salmon steak. Three minutes to prepare and add some grated cheese to the veg to make it tasty.'

'Sounds easy! Are all your meals like that?'

'Oh, I couldn't do that every night—you need more variation than that!'

'That does sound like a bachelor's special. What else do you do?'

Oliver thought about his flat and the mini kitchenette. 'Well, there are only two elements on the stovetop, so I'm a little restricted in what I can cook. There's no way the oven would take a whole turkey, for example.'

'Would it take a roast chicken?'

'Oh yes, it would, but not enough room for all the roast vegetables as well, so I would have to do them in turns. So what do you recommend when someone lives off takeaways?'

Zara paused before answering. 'Well, I'd have to figure out why they were doing takeaways so often. If they don't know how to cook, that leads to a different approach than if they do know how to cook and just don't want to.'

'So if they don't know how, you recommend they go to a few cooking classes or get one of those food bag things?'

'Exactly! It's actually easier if that's the case. It's much harder if they know how to cook but just don't want to.'

'Why's that?'

'Because if they are getting takeaways because they've fallen into bad habits, those bad habits are harder to break. But you can certainly do it. You just have to swap the bad habits for good ones. Regularly going for a walk is the simplest. Then building on that. Go for longer walks. Or going to the gym to spice things up. Just keep doing that each day to build up that regular habit.'

'And for cooking?'

'I like day-of-the-week patterns because people tend to lock themselves into those. So if you say that they can have takeaways one night a week, you might get resistance, but if you say that Saturday night is takeaway night, you're already getting people working on a weekly schedule, and they will find it easier to plan the week's meals. And, therefore, if they know that they're having fish pie on Wednesday, and they have the ingredients already, then they are far less likely to get takeaways on Wednesday as well.'

Oliver gave her an appraising look. 'So how much of your job is actually psychology?'

Zara snorted. 'It's about fifty-fifty. Being a PT is as much about understanding what people think and behave as it is about the actual physicality of exercise. Otherwise, everything I do could be replaced by a list of exercises or a YouTube video.'

Oliver recalled the other PT profiles that he'd seen. 'And I guess the YouTube video wouldn't be yelling encouragement at you during the sessions, would it?'

'I let the other PTs do the yelling. I find that a kind word works better than all the yelling.'

'I'm glad to hear that!'

Chapter 11

ZARA

Kate's attempts at setting Zara up, while fruitful, hadn't netted anyone she particularly even wanted to have a coffee with, let alone take to a wedding. Zara had been getting a steady stream of men ringing her at all hours. In the end, she'd stopped answering her phone and just let them go to voicemail. God knew what her mum had been saying, but from the expectant tone of the messages and some of the comments, she was getting the strong impression they expected her to sleep with them in return for accompanying her to the wedding. It was starting to feel distinctly like her mother was pimping her out. She couldn't help feeling dejected about it all.

At the end of Oliver's midweek session, he was cooling down with a jog on the treadmill, and they were making light conversation about the weather. He'd been a fantastic client so far. Always on time, never grumbling about the exercises she gave him to do, and even did the extra training she'd suggested on the days in between. She knew a large part of his motivation was to get fit so he could travel and also indulge now and then in treats. But she couldn't help wondering if it was also to impress her. She'd caught him gazing at her a few times when he thought she wasn't looking. But he'd never been openly flirtatious, and for that, she was grateful. She'd hate to hurt his feelings by having to ignore it, or worse, give him the 'I don't go out with clients' spiel. Unfortunately today she was in a particularly low mood and less of her chirpy self, so he'd been glancing at her more often, like he sensed something was up and was curious but didn't want to openly pry.

'So what are you up to for the rest of the evening?' he asked her as he switched to a walk, puffing slightly.

'Ignoring phone calls from dodgy men,' Zara said dryly, unable to help herself.

'Huh?'

Zara gave a short laugh and brought down her speed to keep pace with him. 'It's not what it sounds like. A friend's wedding is coming up soon, and I need a plus-one. My mother has taken it upon herself to give every guy she meets my number and ... well, from the messages they're leaving, they sound awful.'

Oliver looked amused. 'No one from the gym you can

take?' He glanced around and happened to spy Jase in the middle of a workout with a client off to the side. He was demonstrating hand-weight exercises, and his bicep muscles bulged. 'What about him? He looks your type.'

'No!' Zara said hastily, 'He's a colleague. And he's not my type.'

'Well, what about me?'

'You?'

'Yeah. I'm happy to help out if you're stuck for someone to take,' Oliver said casually. 'Hopefully you've spent enough time with me by now to know I'm not dodgy.'

Zara was silent. It wasn't like the thought hadn't crossed her mind several times during the past few weeks. She did enjoy Oliver's company. He talked to her like a normal person, not like he was trying to get into her knickers. But still, he was a client.

As she wrestled internally with herself and Oliver waited for her answer, she knew her silence was becoming awkward. Glancing at him, she saw a hot blush forming on his cheeks that was nothing to do with his workout. He really did seem to want to help her out of a fix, and he wasn't just being polite. She knew she was going to regret saying this, but …

'OK, thanks, that would be cool,' Zara replied.

'I think I'm going to need a more formal invitation than that,' he said, blowing out his cheeks, obviously relieved that she hadn't said no.

Zara pushed the stop button on her treadmill and faced him. 'Oliver Staines. Would you do me the honour of accompanying me to Amanda and Eli's wedding at De Vere Latimer Estate in Chesham?'

'Oh. I didn't realise it would be outside London. I thought it was like a registry office or something,' said Oliver, sounding worried.

'Are you backing out?'

'No, no, of course not.'

'There's more. I'm a bridesmaid, so I won't be sitting with you at the reception dinner.'

'Where will I be sitting?'

'I'm not sure. Probably with Uncle John. I hope you like trains.'

'O ... K.'

'It's just for the meal and speeches. I'll check on you periodically. Before the dancing starts.'

'Dancing?' Oliver's face went pale. Zara mentally kicked herself for giving away too much information. Now she'd actually asked him, she didn't want to lose him as a plus-one.

'We don't have to do that,' she said hurriedly. 'We can hang out in the library and drink cognac or something.'

She saw him visibly relax. 'It's a lovely venue,' she continued, trying to reassure him further. 'And it's an overnight stay. Separate rooms, of course. But they look out onto fields and there's a pool and we'll be having a special breakfast buffet the next morning.'

'Oooh, a breakfast buffet,' said Oliver grinning at her. 'Now you're talking.'

Sure enough, just as Zara suspected she might, Fiona had squashed her hot tub in the Thames idea flat as a pancake as soon as she got wind of it. She said it was irresponsible, what if the bride contracted some horrific disease from the water? Zara had pointed out that the water in the tub was clean, and the company had had excellent reviews on Trustpilot. But no, Fiona wasn't keen. The silent disco was even less well received. What if the bride got run over?

Which was why she found herself seated in a room with five other girls on a Saturday afternoon, making a garden in a jar. Zara wished she'd ordered a stripper to waltz in just to see the look on Fiona's face.

Amanda, seated next to her, looked as if she was having as much fun as she was. Namely, none. Looking around, the only person who seemed enthralled was Fiona. She'd already asked half a dozen questions causing the female instructor to drone on about the history of terrariums and the science behind it. Zara yawned and looked at her Fitbit watch.

'What time does this finish again?' she whispered to

Amanda.

'Hopefully soon. I'm about to nod off,' Amanda whispered back, earning a snigger from Zara. Fiona shot them a baleful glare.

They all had high tea in a nice restaurant afterwards, then Zara and Amanda shared a cab to the nearest Tube, clutching the terrariums in their laps.

'So that was the hen do,' said Zara neutrally.

'It was nice. Pleasant, in fact. I'm glad it wasn't a drunken brawl or anything, and at least I got a terrarium out of it. That's cool.'

They passed by the Tube station, and Zara waited to see if Amanda realised. Eventually she cottoned on. 'Hey, where are we going?'

'You'll see.'

They reached West India Quay in Canary Wharf and pulled up outside a shed with a sign saying Hot Tub Boat.

'What? No!'

'Yup. My treat.'

Amanda hugged her. 'Oh my God. You're the best! But I don't have my swimming costume?'

'I've brought along a spare bikini for you. Oh, there's our captain.' A good-looking guy wearing a sailor's uniform was lurking near the shed, trying to appear inconspicuous.

'He looks like a stripper!' Amanda cackled.

Zara laughed along with her, not wanting to spoil the second part of the surprise.

'Just please don't post any photos on Facebook,' she said. 'Fiona will be livid.'

Chapter 12

OLIVER

Oliver owned a custom-made suit that he'd had made by a mate who was doing a tailoring course on Savile Row. In exchange for buying the materials, he'd received a fine single-breasted wool suit in an almost-black navy blue with a lovely gold lining and simple buttons. And then Covid came and work went online and nobody even cared if you were wearing trousers on a Zoom call. Then his body had changed, and he hadn't worn it for years. So when Zara asked him to the wedding, Oliver went home, showered and then tried on the suit. He held his breath as he slipped on the trousers. If the jacket didn't fit, he could kind of get away with it by keeping it unbuttoned, but there would be no escaping sitting in a pair of suit trousers split along the ass seam if he hadn't lost enough weight to fit into them.

He pulled them up and clasped the button at the top of the fly. They seemed to fit OK, even when he let out his breath and stopped sucking his gut in. Even though his body ached all the time, and the treadmill was a constant source of pain, he'd definitely lost weight. He gingerly tried a squat, ears straining to hear any tears. Nothing. He nodded to himself: this was looking promising. It was well known that weddings were a great place to meet single women. There was something about being at an entire event celebrating the awesomeness of a particular relationship that made those without a relationship more receptive to getting into one. Or at least getting a date.

Oliver looked at the invite again. The chapel where the wedding was being held was on the grounds of a hotel just outside the M25. While the M25 was supposed to designate the edge of Greater London, it wasn't materially different on one side of the motorway from the other: it wasn't like you took a single step from idyllic pastures and countryside to barren industrial wastelands belching toxins to the air. Oliver had been assured by Zara that his accommodation had been taken care of by those planning the wedding, so he had little to do pre-wedding except make sure that he knew where he was going and what time he needed to be there.

The ceremony was in the afternoon, so on the big day, he made the one-and-a-half-hour journey via train and a taxi out to De Vere Latimer Estate and dropped off his bag at reception. The ceremony was scheduled before the official check-in time, and his enquiry about an early check-in was gently rebuffed.

He wandered the short distance from reception across the perfectly manicured lawns to the on-site chapel alone, being sure to arrive a solid fifteen minutes before the event. There was no way he would be the last embarrassed guest shuffling down the aisle while the congregation craned their necks to see the bride. Rude! It would be one way of making sure that everyone saw him, but he would never want to be the guy who ruined the once-in-a-lifetime event, the one who made it all about them, causing people to mutter, 'Who's the dipshit upstaging the bride on her special day?'

Being the plus-one for someone in the wedding party was not going to be a good time. He would be alone for the ceremony and the gap between when the wedding party went off to have their photos. And a good portion of the reception. He had his phone, but he was still looking at a lengthy, boring time without anyone to talk to. Still, there would be an open bar and maybe even the opportunity to meet some single women around his age. And Zara would look great in whatever she was wearing, even if it was a bridesmaid's dress. So definitely worth putting up with a bit of boredom.

There were a lot of people in typical wedding gear, summer frocks, fascinators, suits and a bunch of kids running around as well. A giant tree provided some shelter out the front of the church, the sun impressively strong for the early afternoon. Ten minutes before the ceremony started, the vicar came out and invited everyone to come inside and have a seat. Oliver looked around just in case he could spot Zara, but the bride's half of the wedding party were obviously still on their way. He respectfully shuffled into the church, slotting into a pew halfway down the aisle and moving all the way to the end. He didn't know which side was the bride and which was the groom, and since he didn't know either, he figured it wouldn't matter too much.

The church filled reasonably quickly, and before he knew it, he was standing with everyone else and smiling at the ripple as the bride slowly came down the aisle. She looked radiant, and her father, a silver fox guiding her down the aisle, tried to wipe tears from the edge of his eye with a handkerchief.

But Zara had been the one who caught his attention before the bride arrived. The bridesmaids were all in silver silky dresses that fell to the floor, cinched at the waist with a pleasingly plunging neckline. While the others in the party somehow managed to look gawkish, Zara looked like she had stepped off the pages of a magazine. Not that she was tall and thin, rather she moved as if she was at ease being watched. She seemed self-assured, whereas the others in the wedding party were all nervy and self-conscious.

The ceremony seemed to take forever, thanks to a poem read out by the chief bridesmaid. Then the drone of the vicar plus the lack of air circulation made a doubly stuffy environment, and one or two of the older gents nodded off at the back of the church, their gentle snores not quite making it all the way to the front. The vicar had a way about him, a slight nasally whine when speaking, which led Oliver to have to concentrate way too hard to follow what he was saying, and so naturally enough, his mind wandered. The seats were plain wooden pews, but there were cushions for those kneeling slotted into the back of the seats in front. It didn't take Oliver too long before he figured he could use one of those as a cushion for his butt.

The plate-glass windows along the walls were impressive stained-glass scenes from the Bible. All Oliver could think of was what they would look like if someone came swinging through them like a scene out of a movie. They would shatter and the glass would go over everyone and whoever had come through it ... Keanu Reeves, perhaps? He'd charge up to the front of the church, shaking shards of multicoloured glass out of his perfectly coiffed hair. His love interest would be at the front, wearing something haute couture and barely there, and she would look confused before he plunged a sword through the groom, who would naturally enough explode into dust as it turns out he was some sort of non-human creature which would naturally justify such violence. Of course, if the non-humans were accepted into society and she already knew who he was, our mate Keanu would be facing hate-crime homicide charges; now that would be a twist, right?

His mind wandering further, he scanned the part of the congregation in front of him. The vicar droned on further about the nature of love and how the path to love is never smooth and that there would always be challenges and conflicts to be navigated.

Oliver frowned, wondering if the vicar was married and if this speech was something which was trotted out at every wedding or if it actually came from his experience. And if people even needed vicars to tell them about the challenges. And if they needed vicars to bless weddings. There were plenty of celebrants who didn't dress in robes. Ah, but those celebrants didn't come with a nifty church which could be the venue for the ceremony, right? So even if you couldn't abide by the religious mumbo-jumbo, if you wanted the church for the ceremony, you had to pay the piper. Or vicar. It was funny, though. If it wasn't for weddings and funerals and christenings, the church would likely remain empty; religion was out of fashion nowadays. And it was doubly funny; the only way to get anyone to listen to his sermons was for the vicar to say, 'You can't use my church unless you listen to my speeches'. They were like that kid in his town in the Midlands who was the only one with a pool. Incredibly popular in summer but less so in winter. Unless the pool was heated!

Chapter 13

ZARA

Gripping her bouquet, Zara scrunched her toes in her too-tight silver shoes and tried to pay attention as Fiona read out a poem to Amanda and Eli that seemed to have a million verses. Amanda had been remarkably calm all morning, even when the flower girls had become bored and started jumping on the bed, and Fiona yelled at them. Zara had promptly been put in charge, but they hadn't listened to her either. The bride's walk down the aisle had gone smoothly with no tripping over, thank God.

She glanced around the church surreptitiously to see where Oliver was sitting. She knew he was here because he'd messaged her when he arrived. Zara had sent a brief reply: *Great, see you after the ceremony* while she was in the midst of hair and make-up. It was so nice of him to do this for her; she really owed him one. Especially since he'd be at the mercy of Amanda and Eli's friends and relatives for a good part of the day. She eventually spied him sitting halfway down the church next to the wall. He was staring up at the stained-glass windows with a small smile on his face and looked like he was in a world of his own. What was he wearing? A suit? She craned her neck to see better and got a finger jab in the back from Melissa behind her. 'Keep still,' she muttered, 'you're ruining the alignment for the photographer.'

'Sorry,' Zara whispered, noting a young guy with floppy blond hair in a corduroy jacket snapping away with a DSLR. She arranged her face in a placid half-smile and tried to look serene.

After Fiona's poem, the ceremony itself didn't take too long. Before she knew it, she was walking down the aisle behind the happy couple and exiting the church into the fine warm afternoon and a flurry of tossed rose petals. Zara tried to find Oliver in the crush but couldn't locate him. She didn't have her phone on her either, so she couldn't message him. He'd just have to fend for himself while they were off having photos taken. At the instruction of the photographer, Fiona rounded up the bridal party. Zara wasn't sure exactly where they were going, but she found out soon enough. The empty field next to the mansion where there was, according to Simon the photographer, 'ample opportunity for kick-ass shots'. He had a couple of the groomsmen carry a large wicker basket between them.

Amanda caught Zara's eye and giggled, tipsy from the

champagne she'd been drinking before and after the ceremony. 'Fun!' she mouthed. Zara smiled back, trying to ignore her aching arches. Who decided walking through a field was a good idea when the bridesmaids were in high heels? Maybe she should just take the blasted shoes off altogether.

'Right, everyone,' said Simon when they were in the field. 'This won't take long if you all cooperate. We want to get some great shots for Amanda and Eli, right? Memories they can look back on and cherish. They've chosen to do a Mad Hatters Tea Party.'

Everyone whooped politely.

'Good. Right, let's get to it. Grab a prop from the basket and try not to pose as such. We want natural-looking shots, but I'll make artistic suggestions if I get inspired.'

There was a rush to the basket, and Zara was the last to get there. All that was left was a small pink cushion. She wasn't quite sure what she was supposed to do, sit down on it? A peel of laughter from Amanda made her look over. Eli was down on one knee in front of her offering her a bunch of plastic carrots.

'Fantastic, Eli,' encouraged Simon, snapping away. Zara stifled a sarcastic snort. When Amanda sobered up, she might not think it was funny having that on her lounge wall. Everyone looked awkward, standing around holding their various pieces of tea party paraphernalia. Where had they found this guy? He seemed a bit amateurish.

They took a number of group wedding shots, using the various props until Simon announced, 'Hey, I've just had a great idea. See that tree?' Everyone nodded. 'Let's set up a fun picnic scene over there.'

When they'd relocated and finished laying a blanket under the tree, Simon looked around. 'Who's the strongest out of the bridesmaids?' he asked. All heads turned in Zara's direction, and she raised her hand tentatively.

'I think it would make a great photo if you were the Cheshire Cat up in the tree.' He laughed delightedly.

Flipping hell, Zara thought. *He can't be serious.* She glanced up at the nearest low-hanging branch. 'I don't think so.'

'Oh, go on, Zara'—Amanda giggled—'you'll be fine. You've got four men on standby to catch you. Including my husband.' She batted her fake eyelashes at Eli. Everyone looked at her expectantly, and Zara felt like she was being a real Debbie Downer.

'I can't exactly climb a tree in this get-up,' she said, indicating her dress, hoping she was going to be let off the hook.

'I'll give you a leg up,' offered Harry, Fiona's husband.

'Thanks, Harry, so nice of you,' Zara said witheringly,

and Harry grinned.

Simon nodded. 'Right, so, Harry, if you could help Zara into the tree. We'll get into position for the shot.'

Zara's stomach plummeted. She wasn't sure this was a good idea. But now everyone was expecting her to do it. Her palms started sweating.

'Don't worry,' Harry said, 'it'll be fine. It's hardly five feet off the ground. You're not likely to do yourself an injury.'

'Easy for you to say,' replied Zara. 'If I injure myself, I'm not exactly a good advertisement for my job. I'm not sure why I have to do it.'

'Because you're the only one who's fit enough to climb a tree. The rest of us are puny weaklings. But you might want to take your heels off.'

Silently she did as he suggested. Harry bent down and laced his hands together, ready for her to put her bare foot into them. All she had to do was grab hold of the branch and haul herself up. While everyone below pretended to drink tea and act the fool. She shook her head.

'Right, we're ready for you, Zara,' called Simon, camera poised. Everyone was posing and waiting for her.

'Come on, I won't peek at your knickers,' said Harry and laughed when she scowled at him.

Here goes nothing, she thought, placing her foot in his hand. Before she knew what was happening, she was flying into the air towards the tree branch and grabbing for it madly. It was definitely more than five feet high!

Luckily she managed to hook her arm over it, grazing the skin on the underside. This was unbelievable. She managed to get her feet up and hung on upside down for dear life. When she looked down, she saw Harry was now lounging on the picnic blanket with a purple velvet top hat on his head and hamming it up for the camera. She had a strong feeling she must look ridiculous.

'Smile, Zara!' shouted Simon. 'You're the Cheshire Cat!'

Zara bared her teeth in a grimace. She could feel her shoulder muscles straining from the effort. Great, she was going to rip a tendon and be out of action at work! How much longer? From her vantage point, she caught sight of someone walking over the field towards them, and her heart started pounding when she recognised the tall figure in a black suit. Oliver! He must've become bored and tried to find her. She saw him taking in the scene, a bemused look on his face. He frowned when he couldn't spot her and came closer. Any second now, he was going to see her hanging from the tree like a sloth! Zara groaned, her face involuntarily flushing. Typically she hated being the centre of attention or doing anything that made her look like an idiot. That was about to change in exactly five seconds. She could feel her legs slipping. Then she was only hanging on by her arms.

'Help!' she cried out. 'I'm going to fall. Someone catch me! Harry!'

'Just let go, Zara, you're really close to the ground, and I put a cushion beneath you,' he called up to her impatiently. 'Just fall onto that.'

What? Zara twisted her head and saw her small pink cushion placed directly under her. It looked like the size of a postage stamp.

Oh God, thought Zara, this isn't going to go well. But there was nothing for it. She couldn't hold on any longer. She let go of the branch and tried to land on the cushion but missed it completely and landed heavily on her left ankle. Pain shot up her leg. She limped around in a circle, tears spouting from her eyes. Everyone was too busy drinking fake cups of tea for Simon, so it was Oliver who came to her assistance. 'Zara, what the hell? Are you OK?'

'I'm fine,' she gasped. She grabbed the hand he held out to steady her.

'Take it easy,' he said when she attempted to walk. Her ankle sparked with pain, and she winced.

'You're hurt.'

'I'm OK. I just landed weirdly on my foot.'

'Why were you up in a tree, for God's sake?!'

'It was for the photo. Mad Hatters Tea Party.' She gestured at Simon, who was busily checking the photos on his camera. He looked over at them.

'Great shot, Zara. It's perfect.' He smiled in satisfaction and gave her a thumbs-up.

'All in the name of art,' she mumbled, feeling stupid. 'Anyway, I thought you'd be happy. If I'm out of action, you're off the hook for the dancing.'

Oliver raised his eyebrows at her and looked annoyed. 'Seriously?'

She peered at him. He seemed to be really pissed off, whether with her or Simon she wasn't sure. Amanda hadn't seemed to notice what had happened. Now she gestured to Zara and pointed to the grass stains on her wedding dress. Zara sighed and pulled a sympathetic face. She was going to have to help her get those out somehow.

'Let's go back,' she said. 'I think the photos are pretty much over.' Oliver silently picked up her shoes for her, and she grasped his arm, leaning on him.

'Can you walk?'

'Yes.'

She caught the strains of a muted conversation between Fiona and Melissa behind them as they made their way across the field to the mansion.

'Who's he? Her boyfriend?'

'Don't think she has one. Must be a random she picked up somewhere.'

'He's cute.'

'Yeah.'

Zara ignored them and tried to avoid stepping on cow pats.

Chapter 14

OLIVER

Man, that redheaded girl was getting on his tits. She was what, ten? Eleven? And a total shit. The other kids at the table were all right. They acted like kids. A few funny voices and dumb dad jokes, and he was the man. The cool adult. But her in the pink dress, she was like little orphan Annie with an attitude. She was ten going on fifteen with a superior air and snarly contempt for the others. She thought that she should have been at the adults' table, and the fact that she was lumped with Oliver meant that the rest of the table took the brunt of her displeasure.

It had started innocently enough with Oliver introducing himself to the kids and then trying to remember their names as they went around the table. When it got to Red's turn, he'd been greeted with an eye roll and dramatic toss of her hair. Her name was Clara, she said.

'Isn't there a cow named Clara? An animated cartoon or

something.' Oliver knew that kids loved cartoons, so he should be on solid ground here.

'Huh, whatever! Is your last name Twist? You're not exactly a starving orphan, are you, Oliver? Oh, please, sir, may I have some more?' Clara mimicked with exaggerated clarity.

Oliver blinked uncertainly. He hadn't meant anything with his comment about the cow, he was just trying to find a connection with the kids. Kids did like cartoons, didn't they? Still, not too late to rescue the conversation. Time to roll out the charm.

'How do you know about Oliver Twist?'

'I'm in theatre, you nonce, we've covered all the classics already.'

'Oh, how long have you been doing that?' he asked.

'Why, are you going to try and be my agent?' She was all hand gestures designed to be seen from the back rows. 'Well, don't bother, I already have one, and I don't need any pedo asking me to do anything to further my career. Hashtag Me Too.'

Oliver blinked and leaned back at the ferocity of the response. He was just trying to be friendly. The other kids were talking amongst themselves, and Oliver decided silence was his best option. At that point the wedding party entered and everybody stood up. He tried to catch Zara's eye as they trooped in but his table was too far back from the main thoroughfare and so she didn't see him.

He looked around for a bottle of wine, but all the other tables had theirs and seeing as his table was occupied by kids, it was obvious that they had missed out. There were two carafes, one of apple juice and one of orange, so he would have to go up to the bar to get anything alcoholic. Oliver had a feeling he would need more than one drink to get through the night. He pushed his seat back and made his way to the bar as the bridal party got served their food first. *Oh, the privileges of rank,* he thought. At least the bar was close to the kiddies' table. The barman looked up as he approached.

'Can I get a beer, please?' he asked.

The barman frowned. 'The bar will start serving after dinner, sir. There is wine on the table until then.'

'But I'm at the kiddies' table. There's no wine on that table.'

'Oh, I can't serve anything until after dinner. If you come back then, I can get you something.'

'You're joking.'

'Rules from the wedding organiser, sorry.'

Oliver was feeling hard done by as he stomped back to the table with a thirst on and his stomach now rumbling. To distract himself from his hunger, he decided to pull out his assortment of magician's tricks. They weren't technically magic tricks, more like dad jokes in physical form. He opened with the 'flying magic finger'. This is when he placed his fists beside each other and rocked them from side to side together. He started with two fingers extended on each fist and built up the tension with a line of patter in the manner of an auctioneer. 'Look at the fingers, look at them, look at them, see them fly. They're going to go from one fist to another, look there are two on each side and a one, and a two, and a three, fly magic finger fly!' And then he would simply retract one finger on his right hand and extend a third on his left hand, triumphantly presenting them to the audience.

Even at the young age of the audience, there were groans at the lameness of the gag. They were grinning, though, so he knew he was getting them onside. The follow-up was the disappearing finger, where he would wiggle the fist with three fingers extended and count down to three and retract one of them with a flourish. And then ask them if they knew where the missing finger had gone. Ignoring the correct answer yelled at him, he reached behind the ear of the kid sitting beside him (not Clara, of course!) and again triumphantly held out a single finger while proclaiming that it had been hiding behind their ear all along.

Again a chorus of amused discontent at the lameness of the magic, but then a barrage of demands for him to watch them do whatever their party trick was. Oliver realised that by doing such lame magic, he had shown that it was OK for any trick to not be any good and still be OK, and all the kids were taking advantage of that to show off in front of an adult. By the time he had watched most of them fumble their way through their tricks, it was their turn to go up for food and for him to address the empty hole in his belly. If he had been smart, he would have grabbed a snack or something for the long period between lunch and the reception.

Oliver trooped up to the food stations with his collection of little people (ignoring the other guests, elbowing each other and pointing and the smiles at the height difference). Filling his plate responsibly, he headed back to the table and started eating. He hadn't realised how well he had done in getting the kids onside until one decided it would be cool to show Oliver what was in his mouth midchew. The sensible response would have been to not even acknowledge the bad behaviour. To turn his head back to his own meal. But Oliver was enjoying his position as cool adult, and so instead responded by showing his tablemate what was in his mouth as well. This apparently was the height of humour, and the table erupted in laughter.

It shouldn't have made Oliver feel so good, being the cool one at the table. He was used to being the one trying to get the laugh in a group setting, but this was the first time he was slaying with such terrible material. The rest of the meal whizzed by, the speeches, dessert and the cutting of the cake completing the official parts with Oliver not even minding the lack of alcohol.

He was about to get up and find Zara when one of the little girls at his table grabbed his hand and led him to the dance floor. After a few awkward dance moves, he showed her how to stand on his shoes instead. She loved that, holding his hands for balance and mostly matching his movements in time with the music. She'd slide off every now and again when he was too enthusiastic with the size of his steps or she zigged instead of zagging. As the song came to an end, he bowed to her and again was about to go searching for Zara when he noticed a queue forming for his dancing services. Ah well, it couldn't hurt to go see Zara after a bit of a boogie with the kids, surely?

Chapter 15

ZARA

Sitting at the top table was great, Zara decided. Not only were they getting their food served first, but she could also keep an eye on Oliver and see how he was getting on. After he'd helped her back to the hotel, they'd parted ways. Oliver had been relegated to the kiddie table since he was a last-minute guest. He'd been surprisingly OK with it. She wasn't sure she would've been if their positions were reversed. But he seemed to love kids. She peeked over at him now making small talk with a little girl with a mop of red curls. They seemed to be getting along famously. *How sweet*, she thought.

The top table was also making her doubly glad she didn't have to walk anywhere. Her ankle had started to throb badly from falling out of the tree. She really should try and get some ice and a bandage for it somehow, otherwise it was going to start swelling. Limping around at the gym next week would not look good. It would suggest to her clients she didn't know what she was doing.

The speeches started and she settled back to be entertained. Harry delivered a funny one full of amusing anecdotes about what he and Eli had gotten up to when they were at school together, which made everyone chuckle. Then Amanda's father got up and opened with, 'The day my little girl was born, I knew she'd be destined for great things …' So Zara knew it was one of those speeches that was going to go on and on. Ten minutes in, and she was twitching, though Amanda seemed to be enjoying it from her pleased expression. Zara glanced over at Oliver again to find him looking straight at her and rolling his eyes. She stifled a giggle.

After the speeches were finished, the tables were moved out of the way, and Amanda and Eli had their first dance. Then everyone else was invited to join in. Zara hobbled over to where Oliver was and discovered him in demand, with half a dozen little girls lining up to stand on his feet. There was a lot of giggling and 'Me next, me next!' going on as he tried to accommodate them. His dancing, she noticed, resembled Herman Munster at a disco, mostly a lot of clomping.

'Having fun?' she asked him.

'Hey,' said Oliver, red-faced from the exertion. 'I was just having a boogie with this lot, but I'll ditch them if you want to dance?'

'Ah, probably not, sorry. My ankle is starting to really hurt. I might go and beg some ice from the kitchen. And see if they have a first aid kit.'

'Do you want to sit down and I'll get it for you?' he asked, attempting to get the latest girl from off his shoes but she clung to him like a limpet.

'No, no. It's fine. It looks like you've got your hands, or should I say feet, full.'

After locating the kitchen and asking the Spanish chef for some ice and a bandage, Zara ended up getting waylaid chatting to him about nutrition plans since he was training for a marathon in Barcelona. He was around her age, into fitness, single and not bad looking either, she decided. OK, he lived out of London, but long-distance might work if they were both invested in the relationship? And having a boyfriend who could cook was definitely a bonus. However, a server then asked for a round of hot chocolates for the older folk. So she didn't get his name or swap numbers. *Probably a good thing*, she thought, as she made her way back to the main reception room. It was bad form for her to be trying to get a date when she was here with Oliver.

When Zara came into the room, the party was in full swing. Everyone was up and dancing and even a conga line had started, led by Harry, no less. Behind him, Amanda had grabbed onto his waist and looked like she was having a ball kicking out her legs and wiggling her hips.

Zara couldn't see Oliver in the conga line. Fiona and Melissa were sitting down having a breather, so she went over.

'Hi, have you seen my plus-one—Oliver?' she asked, bending close to make herself heard over the music.

'Yeah,' said Melissa. 'Something happened with one of the children. Her mother had words with him, and he went off.' She exchanged a furtive look with Fiona.

'Do you know where?'

She shrugged. 'His room?'

Zara's stomach clenched. Oh no. She shouldn't have left him alone with the kids. Hopefully it was nothing too bad. Or embarrassing. The bag of ice she was carrying was starting to drip on the carpet, so she gave a tight-lipped smile and backed away. She heard them giggling together as she walked off, like they knew exactly what had gone on.

But it was only when she was in the corridor again, faced with a line of closed doors that she realised she didn't actually know which room was his. And her phone was in her room so she couldn't message him.

Zara sighed and headed to her own room that she was sharing with one of the flower girls, Olivia. She'd grab her phone and send him a message from there, then ice her ankle, which was smarting like hell. So much for a fun wedding, it was turning out to be literally a right royal pain, thanks to Simon the photographer's suggestion she climb a tree. She wholeheartedly blamed him and didn't feel guilty at all. Hopefully Amanda didn't notice she wasn't actually there.

Swiping her keycard, she pushed open the door to find a black duffle bag sitting on the other bed. The sound of running water came from the ensuite bathroom. Zara frowned. What the? The door opened, and Oliver came strolling out and stopped in his tracks when he saw her.

'How did you get in here?' he asked, a look of surprise on his face.

'I could ask you the same question,' Zara replied, noting that Oliver had changed out of his suit and was wearing a grey baggy tech t-shirt and jeans. He'd obviously given up on the reception.

'I thought you said we were in separate rooms,' he said, nonplussed.

'So did I! There must've been some mix-up. I'm supposed to be in with Olivia.'

'They must've got confused with Oliver and Olivia. Shall I go and sort it out?'

Zara sighed, feeling overwhelmingly tired all of a sudden. She'd been up since six, so it had been a long day. 'No, don't worry. Olivia must've been put in with Fiona on the pullout couch. At least it's separate beds.' As soon as the words were out of her mouth, she realised it sounded rude. Quickly she added, 'I mean, not that sharing a bed with you would be horrible,' and blushed when Oliver grinned. 'You know what I mean!'

'It's OK, I get it. Besides, I can't promise I wouldn't fart in my sleep or anything. I ate a lot of blue cheese from that gigantic cheese wheel.'

Oliver clutched his throat and made a gagging sound, and Zara laughed.

'Maybe we should keep the window open, so I don't get gassed in the night,' she joked.

'That's not a bad idea,' said Oliver seriously. 'I see you got some ice for your ankle.'

'Yeah.' Zara held up the dripping bag and didn't mention the Spanish chef. 'They even had a bandage, so I'm sorted. Might be a bit of swelling tomorrow but it should be OK if I get this on it pronto. I should probably use the bathroom and get changed.'

Oliver nodded.

Zara unzipped her wheelie and grabbed her toiletry bag. This was awkward! She *knew* inviting Oliver to the wedding was going to be problematic. She shouldn't have bothered. It wasn't like they'd spent any time together at the wedding and now they were forced to spend the night together in the same room. It was a level of intimacy she wasn't sure she was ready for. Especially when rifling through her clothes, she realised she'd only brought a skimpy black negligee to wear to bed. She hurriedly stuffed it back in and pulled out a t-shirt and leggings instead. She'd been planning to go for a run before breakfast but her injured ankle had put paid to that.

Oliver was lying on the other twin bed scrolling when she came out of the bathroom, face scrubbed clean of make-up and teeth brushed. Zara couldn't help but notice his arms had more muscle definition than when they'd started working out together. She opened her mouth to say something but then closed it again. If she started going on about his biceps, it could be construed as a come-on.

She sat on her bed and propped her ankle on a pillow, spread a towel over it and dumped the ice on top. At last, though it was practically melted now.

'So why did you come back to the room?' she asked, leaning back against the headboard. 'Did something happen?'

Oliver didn't reply immediately. A slow flush crept up his neck. 'Let's just say one of the kids' mothers didn't want her child dancing with me. Parents are a bit overprotective these days.'

'What do you mean?'

Oliver sighed. 'Little Orphan Annie told her mother I was a pedo. Of course word got around.'

Zara jerked upright and looked at him. 'What? The redheaded girl? That's ridiculous. You were being nice to the kids!'

'I know.' Oliver pursed his lips and looked annoyed. 'She had it in for me from the start. We had words at the table.'

'Here I was thinking you were getting on great with her!'

Oliver shook his head emphatically. 'No! She's a theatre kid. A real little madam.'

Zara stifled a laugh at that. 'God, that's awful,' she said. 'I'll talk to her mother tomorrow and sort it out. You don't want to have that hanging over you.'

'Thanks. I'd appreciate it.'

Zara thought back to what he'd told her about the various incidents at the gyms. 'You do seem to have an interesting life.'

Oliver shrugged. 'Let's just say things tend to happen to me. And it's mostly not my fault.'

Chapter 16

OLIVER

The lights were off, and they were in the hotel room, each on their own single bed. Not quite how Oliver wanted to be sleeping with Zara in a hotel room. Never mind, putting those thoughts out of his mind, he stared at the ceiling. He'd just told her about the incident with the Clara kid, and she'd believed him when he told her that it was perfectly innocuous. Rather than dwell on the more recent situation, he wanted to talk about something else. Anything else.

'So what embarrassing incident at my old gym are we up to?' he asked, half turning in the darkness.

'I think you've told me about the metal water bottle as a missile on the treadmill ... and the Dyna-Band hitting you on the treadmill. That's my favourite one so far. You don't have much luck on treadmills.'

'OK, just remember with that one that I was the victim. Falling at that speed could have really hurt!' He sensed her disbelief in the dark. 'OK, maybe there wasn't too much speed ... but still. I'll give you another one. And this one was really not my fault. Seriously, just the wrong place at the wrong time. I had entered the gym and was walking to the treadmills after stretching. They had foolishly put one of the weight machines, the one with the cables and pulling handles, right on the corner.'

'Why was that a problem?'

'Well, when someone is using it they have their hands at their sides, but when they do the exercise, they are pulling their leg or arm away from the weight into the corridor where people are walking. And with some great force. It's fine when they're facing you, but half the time they're doing one side and the other half the time they're facing the other way doing the other side. So half the time they can see you coming and half the time they can't—coin toss. And if you happen to be walking along as they do an arm exercise without warning, you get punched in the head, and if they are doing a leg exercise, you get kicked instead.'

'And so you kicked someone?'

'Oh, no! I was walking past, and there was someone walking towards me. The girl on the machine was doing legs and kicked out as the guy was walking past, and he went flying into me.'

'So really not your fault.'

'Yeah, but there was a report and a talk and they made a little note on my record.'

Zara finished the phrase with him, and they both laughed. For better or worse, it seemed to be a catchphrase for them.

The next morning they headed down to the restaurant after a light workout session in the hotel gym. Zara had done some yoga since her ankle was still sore. Oliver was hungry and looking forward to the main event—the breakfast buffet. He could leave the wedding weekend with a full belly and pleasant memories rather than with a bad taste in his mouth from the reception. Last night's conversation with Zara had gone a long way to achieving that; she was very easy to talk to and didn't give him a hard time for his missteps and fumbles. He sometimes forgot what a knockout she was, but even in the morning, in casual clothes and a five-minute make-up session in the bathroom, she was incredibly presentable. Weren't beautiful girls supposed to be princesses with multi-hour beauty regimes? Movies were always showing the guy waiting around forever for them to get ready.

Zara laughed out loud as he grinned and rubbed his hands when he saw the spread on offer for breakfast. He scanned the tureens and catering dishes, planning his first plate. You had to go with the full English to start with, surely? Hash brown, eggs two ways (scrambled and fried), mushrooms, a sausage and a pair of rashers of bacon. He dropped his plate off at their table and asked if Zara wanted any juice.

Around them was a sprinkling of guests from the wedding; the rest of them must still be in bed or have left late last night. He couldn't see anyone from his table, thankfully.

Zara was keeping things low calorie, cereal with yoghurt and fruit. She turned down the offer from a waiter of a coffee and only had the grapefruit juice that Oliver had fetched for her. Oliver, on the other hand, got a coffee as well. That was the great thing about Zara—she was never judgy; she didn't even raise an eyebrow at his breakfast consumption. Oliver was a great convert to her concept of 'don't sweat the exceptional days as long as your regular eighty percent was healthy'. She'd corrected him when he had used the term 'cheat day'. 'How can it be cheating if you're just having the twenty percent day? It's not cheating if it's following the rules, right?'

'I guess so, like an open marriage, right?'

She'd rolled her eyes. 'I guess!'

Oliver watched her as he hoovered up his cholesterol plate of fun, chasing the fried egg yolk around the plate with the last of the hash brown. *She was great*, he thought, *hot, clever and really nice*. If he wasn't paying to spend time with her, maybe things would be different. And maybe if he was on the other side of his fitness journey. She probably had guys at the gym lining up around the block for a date; why would she want to go out with him? Typical fate, giving him the perfect girl when he wasn't anywhere near maximum studliness himself. Ah well …

He got up, smiling as Zara looked up in surprise.

'Cheat day,' he sang softly to her as he made his way back to the buffet.

Round Two!!

The waffle station had a sign indicating it was *For the kids.* It had a self-serve machine where you poured a pre-measured amount of batter onto the waffle grill, and a timer counted down the time as the waffle cooked. Oliver ignored the sign. Breakfast was for everyone, surely? While he waited for his waffle, he collected the condiments that he would require, butter and maple syrup in small single-serve sachets and a pair of giant marshmallows because, why not? He contemplated getting a couple of pancakes too, which were baking under the heat lamps, but the edges were browning, and they looked dry, and he didn't want to come across as a glutton. Zara might have been off the table as far as potential girlfriends go, but he didn't want her thinking of him as a pig!

Chapter 17

ZARA

Oliver slung his duffle bag over his shoulder and picked up Zara's wheelie and carried it to the waiting taxi. She saw him frown, watching her limp down the steps and had a flash of intuition that he was thinking of carrying her as well. But he said nothing. Just stood waiting with the door open for her, and she pushed the fleeting thought aside feeling silly. Ensconced in the taxi, they weaved down the narrow country lanes heading towards Chalfont & Latimer station. She'd arranged with Erin to pick her up from Preston Road so she didn't have to navigate getting to Ealing with her luggage. She assumed Oliver would stay on the train into the city.

After getting on so well last night, she was surprised to find she felt awkward with him. Was he a client, were they now friends, or ... something else? She wasn't sure. They'd talked for a while after the lights were off, and she'd learned he was originally from Coventry and his mother had passed away from breast cancer while Oliver and his sister, Anne, were at high school. Then he'd gone off to university in London. He'd asked about her family, and she'd told him about her dad dying and how difficult it had been. His sympathy hadn't been fake because he knew exactly how she felt.

Oliver was staring out the window at the passing fields, and she cleared her throat, attempting to fill the silence with neutral ground conversation. 'Ah, so I guess I'll see you on Tuesday for your usual session? I should still be OK to train, I just won't do any treadmill work with you.'

Oliver turned and stared at her. He seemed miles away. 'Huh? Oh! Yes, definitely.' He patted his stomach. 'I did some serious damage on that breakfast buffet, so you'll have to give me a vigorous workout.'

Zara grinned. 'I'm sure I can come up with something. How does fifty burpees and three sets of kettle bells sound?'

Oliver groaned. 'Horrific.'

'You can handle it. You're getting some real strength and definition in your biceps now.'

'Am I?' Oliver sounded surprised and looked down at his arms. He was wearing another tech logo t-shirt, a dark blue one this time.

Zara bit her lip. Dammit, she wasn't supposed to mention his arms. 'Er, yes. You're really making progress.'

Oliver shrugged. 'I'm not really fussed about muscles, remember. I just want to get fit.'

'Yes, of course. How you feel is more important. How *do* you feel?' she asked curiously, realising she'd never really asked him that. She just assumed because he looked fitter he must be feeling it.

'Overall I feel great!' he said, beaming at her. 'I'm up and down the stairs at work like a whippet, and I hopped on the scales before I left to come here and I've lost two stone. I'm chuffed at that. One is usually my limit, then I pile it all back on again. We must be doing something right.'

'That's awesome!'

'Yeah. It's mostly because of you, so thanks.'

'Rubbish,' Zara replied, brushing aside the compliment. 'You've done the hard work. I'm just there to provide guidance and motivation.'

'No, I mean it. Seriously—thank you.' Oliver's warm brown eyes fixed on her own, and Zara felt a small zing in her solar plexus that was hard to ignore.

'By the way, I sorted your issue,' she said, averting her gaze.

'My issue?'

'You know, the pedo thing.'

Oliver's cheeks flushed. 'Oh yeah.'

'The little madam won't be going around saying things

like that again,' Zara said confidently. In reality she hadn't known what to say specifically. But she'd had an inkling of an idea and cornered the redheaded girl when she saw her go into one of the bathrooms in the hallway after breakfast. When she came out, Zara told her that it was very wrong she'd told her mum Oliver was a pedo and she needed to tell her he wasn't. The kid had put her hands in her pinafore pockets and smirked. 'I don't know what you're talking about.'

Zara had said that was a pity because she knew people in the musical theatre business (well, Erin had watched enough to qualify) and they didn't like liars. A certain redheaded girl might find herself being passed over for roles if she didn't tell her mum the truth. Funnily enough, after hearing that, the girl had been more compliant, almost grovelling, and said she would talk to her mother immediately.

'Thank God,' said Oliver, sounding grateful, 'what did you do?'

'Just trust me, it's sorted.' Zara patted his hand, and Oliver looked down at her fingers resting on top of his. He seemed about to say something but the taxi pulled into the station just then and the moment was broken with the wrestle of who was paying and retrieving their luggage from the boot. They only had a three-minute wait for the train, and once on board, they had separate seats due to it being nearly full. So there was no further conversation or hand interaction. Unfortunately.

Gazing out the window, Zara admitted to herself that spending time with Oliver had been the highlight of the wedding. Even more than being a bridesmaid and seeing Amanda and Eli get married. She turned her head slightly and saw him on the other side of the carriage facing the window, his strong profile clearly outlined against the pane. Another zing of attraction went through her and Zara sucked in her breath. She really liked him. Maybe she should break her own rule of not dating a client and ask him out? She had a feeling he wouldn't ask her even if he wanted to.

Just before the Preston Road stop, Zara stood up and started elbowing her way towards the door and was about to say 'Bye' to Oliver when he followed her lead. 'Aren't you staying on to Farringdon?' she asked him.

'Nah, I'll help you with your bag and then catch the next one.' She wasn't sure if he was just being a gentleman or if he really wanted to spend a bit more time with her.

'You don't have to if it's a hassle.'

He shrugged. 'I've got nothing urgent to do today. Apart from shopping for a new toaster. Mine has this annoying timer thing which just clicks round and doesn't actually pop the toast. If you don't keep an eye on it, boom!'—he waved his hands upward with a dramatic flourish—'you've got two pieces of inedible charcoal and a flat full of smoke. Not ideal.'

She giggled. 'No, definitely not!' It was on the tip of her tongue to say she'd go with him. But Erin was picking her up, so she couldn't exactly ditch her and go off with Oliver. Besides, she had her wheelie and a sore ankle.

Oliver carried her bag and they walked together to the entrance of the station. Zara spotted Erin's red Fiat a little way along the street. 'That's my ride.'

'Cool. I wonder when the next train is.' Oliver started tapping on his phone. By this time Erin had seen her and gotten out of the car.

'Hey!' said Erin when she was within earshot. 'How was the wedding?'

'It was great, thanks. We had a nice time. It went off without a hitch too, well, apart from the photos.'

She prepared to launch into her story about the Mad Hatter's Tea Party shoot but then noticed that Erin was staring at Oliver, who was still on his phone. She had briefly mentioned to Erin she was taking a client to the wedding but no details about who they were and Erin hadn't asked.

'Oliver, this is Erin, my flatmate,' she said.

Oliver looked up from his phone. 'Hi, Erin, nice to meet you,' he said politely.

'Nice to meet you too,' she said with a smile. 'Did you need a lift somewhere?'

'Ah, I was catching the next train into the city but it seems there's a delay so I guess I'll have to wait. Maybe I can find a shop that sells toasters …' He hitched his bag higher on his shoulder and looked around expectantly to see if there were any.

'I can give you a lift to our flat if you want to Tube it from West Ealing,' offered Erin. 'Saves you waiting around.'

'That would be amazing, thanks, if that's OK?' replied Oliver, looking at Zara, who shrugged.

'Fine with me. We should all be able to squeeze in. You better go in the front, though, since you've got longer legs.'

Zara was squashed with her wheelie in the back seat for the half-hour journey while Erin chatted away to Oliver. Asking him what he did for work, where he lived and what he did on the weekends when he wasn't going to weddings.

Oliver replied readily enough. Zara couldn't tell if he was actually engaged in the conversation or just being polite. He didn't seem to be asking similar questions, but maybe that was because he already knew what Erin did since Zara had briefly mentioned during one of their training sessions that her flatmate was a marketing exec.

When they pulled up outside the flat, Zara extricated herself and her bag onto the pavement. She waited for Oliver to get out so she could point him towards the Tube, but he was listening to something Erin was saying and wasn't moving.

She rapped on the window to get his attention, and Oliver looked up at her with an expression she couldn't quite gauge.

Erin lowered the window and leaned forward. 'I might as well take Oliver into the city,' she called out brightly. 'Seems silly for him to catch the Tube when I've got a full tank.'

Oliver smiled at Zara. 'Thanks again for the wedding invite; I had a great time.'

'Ah,' said Zara, not sure how to react to this abrupt turn of events. 'Good. Me too.'

'See you on Tuesday for my workout?'

'Yes, see you then.'

They drove off, leaving Zara with a bad feeling in her gut.

When Erin arrived back at the flat after dropping Oliver off, she bustled around plumping couch cushions and polishing the leaves of her house plants while singing show tunes from *West End Story* under her breath. The bad feeling Zara had been nursing increased in depth and width. Something had obviously happened to inject Erin with energy but what?

She leaned against the lounge doorjamb, watching her. 'You were gone for a while. Did Oliver give you the wrong directions?' she asked casually.

Erin jumped like a startled cat at his name and flushed bright red.

'No, he got back OK. There was just a bit of Sunday traffic.' She quickly looked down at the dark green plant on the windowsill that she was studiously polishing. Its leaves were now so shiny they reflected the sky outside.

'Did something happen though?' persisted Zara. 'You're acting odd.'

Erin cleared her throat. 'I, ah … and I hope you don't mind … but I may have asked him out. On a date.'

Zara pressed her lips together. Dammit. 'Did he say yes?' She hoped Oliver had thought it was too weird and had declined the offer.

'He did, actually,' said Erin, a touch defensively. 'We haven't arranged it yet, but I thought maybe … a midweek drink.'

'Oh—cool.' Zara tried to smile but it must've not quite reached her eyes.

'You're pissed off,' said Erin looking deflated. 'Because he's your client. I'm really sorry. He just seemed nice. And I asked if he was seeing anyone. He said no.'

Zara rubbed her hand tiredly over her face. Her ankle was starting to ache again—she needed to ice it and wrap it before work tomorrow. She went into the kitchen to raid the freezer, with Erin following her, looking guilty.

'There isn't anything going on with the two of you, is there?'

'Of course not,' said Zara sharply. 'He's a client. Honestly, it's fine that you asked him. And yes, he is a nice guy.'

She yanked the ice tray out of the freezer with more force than necessary. Maybe nothing would happen. They'd just go on one date, find out they had nothing in common and that would be it. Over and done with. And they could all move on with their lives.

Chapter 18

OLIVER

A month later, Oliver bounded up the stairs at the office—they were no longer a threat, and he loved it. He would take a seat in one of the meeting rooms, ready to go, and thirty seconds later he'd be breathing normally, while the others in the room would arrive in dribs and drabs with red faces and puffing and wheezing. He was enjoying the quiet when Sam and Toby walked in.

'Hey, Olly, how was your weekend? Were you fighting the ladies off?' said Toby.

'Actually, no, I've started seeing someone,' Oliver replied.

'That's awesome,' replied Sam. 'Where did you meet her?'

'Or him,' leered Toby.

'I met *Erin*'—Oliver responded with a glance at Toby—'at a friend of a friend's wedding. She gave me a lift home after the reception, and she asked me out. Fast forward four dates, and I asked her to be my girlfriend.'

Toby snorted.

'Yeah, I know! It sounded weirdly high school when I said it too, but she found it endearing, and she said "yes", so here we are.'

'I'm so glad for you,' gushed Sam. 'You kept that very quiet. Why the secret? What's she like?'

'She's ... good. It's early days, so we're still figuring each other out. I didn't want to tell anyone until it felt ... more real, I guess.'

'What is she into? What does she do?'

'Musicals, she likes musicals.'

'What, like show tunes?'

'Yeah. And she's a marketing exec, so lots of talk about campaigns and such.'

Toby rolled his eyes. 'Sounds fun. What about the sex?'

Oliver rubbed his eyes. 'You're a grievance just waiting to happen, Toby. Really?'

Sam stepped in. 'Does she like to travel? You love it so much it would be great to have someone to travel with, wouldn't it?'

Oliver nodded slowly. One thing about travelling on his own was being solo, and it was lonely. And a little more expensive. 'We haven't talked about that yet. I'm sure she will. She's fun.'

Sam nodded uncertainly. 'Yeah, I'm sure ... So I guess this

means that you're off the market?'

Oliver blinked in surprise. 'I guess. Why?'

Sam shuffled her notes. 'Ah, no reason. There was someone in Legal who was wondering what your deal was.'

Toby grinned. 'And what was *his* name?'

Oliver ignored him. 'Well, if they want to go for a coffee, I guess that would be OK.'

Sam frowned. 'Are you sure?'

'Hey, if they want to have a coffee, there's plenty of ole Olly to go around,' he said, making a dancing motion from the waist up in his chair.

A week later, he was at a work function at the local bowling alley. He was torn between two opposing feelings. On one hand, he quite liked a free lunch of pizza on Tuesdays. And lots of his fellow employees liked the Wine Tasting Club. Or the Whisky Tasting Club. And these monthly outings to the bowling alley after work were good innocent fun. But instead of those bitsy efforts at raising morale, he thought that their employer might have been better served focussing on salary adjustments and basic humanity training for the managers. The entire office was invited, and a good number of them made it, though looking around, Oliver noticed it was mainly the younger employees and those without children or others relying on them back home. As he swigged his beer, he wondered how much of the 'fun budget' was spent on events where a lot of the staff would get no benefit from it.

He had arrived late, so his lane consisted of him and two others—basically, the leftovers after everybody else had been organised into teams of six. The other two were wandering between the lanes chatting with people and occasionally returning to the lane to make a half-arsed effort to knock down the pins before leaving on another socialising lap. While Oliver would have loved to rove between the other lanes as well, he'd had a hard leg session the previous day, and walking was a bit of a painful effort, so he settled into the seat, sipping his beer alone. He knew he looked like a Noddy-No-Mates, but he was OK with his own company.

'Hey, Oliver mate, how're things?' Toby flopped down into the seat facing Oliver and took a long swig from his beer. The khaki shorts and t-shirt barely covering his belly just made the bowling shoes look even more clownish.

'Good! How's the bowling going?'

'You mean, how am I scoring?' He guffawed. 'Lousy. Gutter balls with the odd seven or eight to cruelly give me hope. Listen, I hear you took Tabitha from Legal out for a coffee? But you've got a girlfriend, right?'

Oliver frowned, not quite seeing Toby's point. 'Erin, yes, she's my girlfriend. And Tabitha and I just had a coffee; it wasn't anything romantic.'

Toby wasn't listening. 'Yeah, yeah. Right. Anyways, if you've got your girlfriend and Tabitha is throwing herself at you, maybe you could point her my way? Subtly though: maybe indicate that you're surprised that Toby doesn't have a girlfriend. But make it sound like I usually do have a girlfriend, so she knows it's a short-term opportunity which isn't likely to be repeated. So she has to act quickly.'

Oliver blinked and tried to suppress a smile. 'Sure, that sounds like something I could tell her.' He craned his neck and nodded as if in response to a mimed question from the other side of the alley. 'I think it's your turn to bowl in your lane,' he told Toby.

'You're a pal, Olly,' Toby told him as he levered himself out of the seat and headed back into the crowd.

Oliver had just let out a sigh and taken another sip of beer when the building's receptionist, Joelene, arrived unsteadily and sunk into Toby's freshly vacated seat. 'Hi, Olly,' she half-said half-sung. It looked like she had been taking advantage of the open bar while Oliver was finishing off his work before the event.

'Hi, Joelene, how's your evening going?'

'Good now,' she said, giving an exaggerated smile at him, which was more of a leer. Just then, a couple of the executive assistants came over and collected her, almost dragging her bodily away.

'Great event!' he called after them as Joelene protested her abduction. He recalled that one of them had put the whole thing together.

The seat had been vacant for less than thirty seconds when someone else plonked themselves down in it. Oliver looked around to see if there was a queue somewhere. This time it was one of the junior accountants. 'Hi, Maria, isn't it?'

Maria blinked as if surprised at being recognised. 'Yes, hello.' She spoke with a slight German accent. 'You had a coffee with my friend on Monday. But I heard that you have a girlfriend.'

'Is your friend Tabitha or Emily?'

'My friend is Emily.'

'Ah, cool. Yes, I had a coffee with her.'

'But you have a girlfriend?'

'Yes, I do. Erin.'

Maria appeared confused. 'So you are not looking for a girlfriend?'

'No, as I said, I have one already. Erin.'

'Ach, I see.' She stood up. Oliver almost expected her to give a little bow, but she left, the bowling shoes giving little squeaks on the shiny floor.

Oliver wasn't interested in entertaining any more slightly tipsy co-workers, so he left his seat to get another beer. The time sitting still had made the effort to get up even more painful, and he was using the time at the bar, waiting for his beer to contemplate if he would be better served getting some exercise rather than hunkering down in the seat. He was used to not necessarily being fully aware of what was going on socially around him; he suspected he might be somewhere along the autistic scale, and nights like this one were naturally a little confusing. Alcohol helped. He could blame other people's behaviour on alcohol consumption or else drink enough so the confusion was overtaken by intoxication. Win-win!

Chapter 19

ZARA

Technically, her client going out with her flatmate shouldn't bother her. But Erin had muscled in on Oliver when Zara was about to ask him on a date herself. How that might have gone was a different story but she hadn't had a chance to find out. Erin and Oliver had been on a handful of dates, and then he'd frigging asked her to be his girlfriend!

Even worse was that she was getting a blow-by-blow account of their fledgling relationship at home, whether she liked it or not. And being asked her opinion about it. *Oliver hadn't invited Erin to stay over at his flat yet, was that normal? Oliver had said such-and-such, what do you think he meant?*

In the end, she'd had to tell Erin gently that it was breaking the gym's client confidentiality rules for her to comment in any way, shape or form on Oliver's intentions (whatever they may be).

'Huh? Isn't that to do with doctors?'

'It also applies to personal trainers,' explained Zara patiently. She had no idea if it did or not but she couldn't stomach hearing any more about it.

From then on, it was blessed silence on the Oliver front. Apart from Erin's muffled voice on the phone in her bedroom as she relayed their dates to a friend instead. Zara thought she would be better off not knowing anything. But now she found herself straining to hear. Were they on the rocks? Were they serious?

Oliver hadn't mentioned anything about Erin at their training sessions. And she hadn't asked him. It was none of her business what he did in his private life. But it still felt awkward, like they'd formed a friendship during the wedding. And now *this thing* had happened. Zara felt like they should talk about it and clear the air but was supremely reluctant to bring up the topic.

So, when she spotted him in Sports Direct one sunny Saturday morning rifling through a rack of shorts, she almost turned on her heel and left the shop. But figured it would be more awkward if he saw her and wondered why his personal trainer was avoiding him. So she slowly made her way over.

'Hey, what are you doing in Ealing?' she asked, trying not to sound accusing.

Oliver glanced up at her voice and smiled. 'Fancy seeing

you here! I'm just buying some new workout gear, then I'm meeting Erin for a coffee.' This was the first time that Oliver had actually mentioned Erin's name in her presence or acknowledged something was going on, so it felt like a step in the right direction towards transparency. She relaxed a little.

'Right. What's wrong with your usual workout gear?'

'My shorts are starting to fall down, and we don't want any incidents,' he joked.

Zara giggled. 'Or notes being made on your record.'

'Exactly.' He grinned at her. 'What are you getting?'

'Just some training socks.'

Zara waved the socks she was holding in his face, and he batted them away. 'Yuck.'

She laughed at his expression. 'I haven't worn them, silly!'

'Still, it's the principle of the thing,' Oliver replied as they made their way towards the front of the store. 'I wouldn't brandish a pair of men's briefs at you.'

'If they were clean, so what?'

Oliver glanced at her. 'You wouldn't be embarrassed?'

'Not particularly. I'm not easily embarrassed.'

'Hmm.' Oliver had a slightly amused expression, and it sounded like he had a story about someone who had been highly uncomfortable in some sort of underwear situation. She knew that look.

'Annnywaaay ...' said Zara, after he'd told her another one of his amusing gym anecdotes, how many did he have? 'Are you going to try your stuff on?'

Oliver glanced down at the shorts and quick dry performance t-shirt he was holding. 'Yeah, I probably should. I'm not even sure what size I am now. I just took a guess.'

'If they don't fit, I can play assistant and grab you a different size if you like,' Zara suggested helpfully.

He nodded. 'OK, thanks.'

She started flicking through a sale rack of women's t-shirts nearby while Oliver disappeared into the men's changing rooms. He was in there for a good ten minutes, and she started getting bored. She stuck her head into the corridor of cubicles and called out, 'Have you got them on yet?'

'Yes, but they might be a bit tight.'

'Let's have a look then.'

There was silence then an 'OK' floated back to her.

Zara returned to the t-shirt rack and wasn't really paying attention when Oliver came out into the store wearing a fitted grey muscle t-shirt and black running shorts.

He cleared his throat to get her attention. When she looked up, she got the shock of her life. During their months of working out together, Zara had gotten used to seeing Oliver in plus-size clothes—baggy knee-length shorts and loose-fitting tech t-shirts. Even at the wedding, she hadn't had a complete visual of his body. She knew he'd lost a bit of weight, but now she realised she'd been inadvertently blindsided. The guy standing before her was definitely not overweight anymore. He was tall and toned and could give any of the PT guys in the gym a run for their money. She blinked. Then blinked again. Realising her mouth was slightly hanging open, she snapped it shut.

Oliver plucked the t-shirt away from his flat stomach. 'Does it look OK? It feels quite tight. And I'm not used to wearing such small shorts. It feels like my legs are on display.'

She was amazed that he had to ask. Did he not look in the dressing room mirror? Maybe there wasn't one.

Zara realised he was waiting for her opinion, so she tried to sound professional. 'Uh, I think they fit pretty well.'

A fake-tanned female sales assistant in a white Nike crop top and black leggings sashayed over. 'Can I help you with anything?' she purred. A badge over her boob read Natasha.

'He was just trying some workout gear on for size. I'm his PT,' explained Zara feeling a touch of pride. Why she felt she had to add that she didn't know. Maybe because he was looking damn hot, and she wanted to show Natasha that she'd had a hand in his fitness journey.

But the assistant's attention was firmly fixed on Oliver. 'Well, I think they both fit perfectly,' she stated, giving him a once-over. 'Did you want to get them?'

Oliver looked at Zara, who nodded and gave him a thumbs-up. 'Guess I will then,' he said with a smile. He walked off jauntily back into the changing room, and Zara noticed Natasha watching his taut butt.

'His PT *and* his girlfriend. Wow, you're lucky,' she murmured and went off back to the counter before Zara had a chance to correct her. Her words hit home, though. Now she knew exactly why Erin had pounced on Oliver and what she'd lost out on. He was the complete package—brains, brawn AND personality.

But she'd had ample opportunity. Why hadn't she flirted with him at the wedding, told him he looked hot in his suit or something? They'd slept in the same room together, for crying out loud! Surely she could've engineered a back rub! She'd held back for the sake of propriety. Now it was too late. Even if there had been a glimmer of hope with him as her client, as Erin's boyfriend, he was well and truly off-limits.

Chapter 20

OLIVER

Bumping into Zara at the shop was an unexpected bonus. Oliver hated clothes shopping, always had. When he was younger, he had been a bean pole and weirdly proportioned so that nothing fit well. His torso was too long, so normal t-shirts were too short, and if he got the length right, then there would be too much sag in the chest, making him look like he was in some sort of dress. Gaining weight during Covid meant he had only very briefly passed through a pleasing shape before coming out the other end. And then he hated shopping for a totally different reason. Now? Well, he should have been revelling in his transformation, but the memory of all the bad experiences in the fitting rooms came flooding back. So having a friendly face to alleviate the pain would be good. It would take the sting out of 'I'm sorry, they don't have anything in your size.'

But he was pleasantly surprised; the clothes seemed to fit.

OK, a little tighter than he normally wore them, but that seemed to be more about the style rather than too much Oliver in not enough clothing.

The sales assistant seemed nice, too; instead of hiding out the back doing her nails or chatting with her colleagues, she actually seemed interested in helping. Until Zara popped up anyways. And then she kept her distance, but whenever he looked at her, she was looking over, making sure he didn't need any help. Friendly!

Zara was good value. She mentioned something about underwear, which made him remember a humorous story he only just stopped himself from telling her.

The story was that he and Erin had decided to stay in at his place and ordered a pizza. The website said that they had forty minutes, so they had decided to put that time to good use. But the pizza had not taken as much time to cook as the website had suggested. Or maybe the delivery guy had found a shortcut. Whatever. They'd both been naked when the doorbell rang. Oliver had hastily dressed, only noticing that he had inadvertently scooped up Erin's underwear as he hurriedly pulled them on. His robe was thrown on in a rush as well and he was pretty sure that the delivery guy got a glimpse of the black lace. And his todger sticking out. Women's G-strings did not provide much support for the male anatomy. Funny that. Not the sort of story to tell Zara, that's for sure!

She had looked at him expectantly, so he had to tell her some story, so instead he told her one of his gym stories.

'You must work at a lot of gyms, right?'

'Sure ...?' Zara responded.

'So they all have their own colour schemes, right? Red for Virgin Gyms, orange for EasyGyms and so on?'

'OK.'

'So at my old gym, they have a particular shade of light blue. Very unusual. And for Christmas a couple of years ago I got a three-pack of gym shirts from my stepmother. One was black, one was green and one was the exact colour that the staff wore at my gym. I didn't think anything of it; I mean, it registered—hey, that's the same colour as the staff shirts. Oh well.' He could see that Zara was putting one and one together.

'Oh, no.'

'So one day I wore that shirt. And nothing happened.' Zara looked suspicious. 'And the next week nothing happened either. But then the third time I wore it, a guy was using a machine and asked me if I thought he would be able to do eighty kilo if he could bench sixty kilo. I shrugged and said sure, why not? I didn't realise that he was asking me because he thought I knew what I was talking about. He thought I was a staff member. But my shirt didn't have staff written on it, it was just the same colour.'

'What happened?'

'I heard this terrible crash, there was yelling, and the guy was in a lot of pain. Anyway, there was a report, and a talk, and they made a little note on my record.'

Oliver paid for the clothes, turning down the kind offer of signing up for the store credit card if he provided Natasha with his email address, and turning down the warranty if he provided her with his phone number. He was feeling pretty pleased with the whole experience as he and Zara left the store.

'Do you want to come for coffee with me and Erin?' he asked.

Zara looked a little distracted. 'No, I've got things to do, tell her I said hi, though.'

'Will do,' Oliver said and headed towards the cafe.

He got there before Erin and ordered their drinks. He was proud of the fact that he remembered what she liked (decaf soy mocha), and while he waited, the barista seemed quite keen on having a chat. She was tall and slim and had brown eyes, which she had heightened with smoky eyeshadow and eyeliner. When she spoke to him it was in accented English.

'Would you like to come out to see a new band? They're supposed to be, as you English say, the tits.'

'Your accent is awesome. Where are you from?'

'Milano,' she answered, dimples appearing at the corners of her mouth. She had a habit of looking up through her fringe at him. And then flicking the fringe out of her way so she could see the coffee making.

'Cool, when are they playing?'

'I'll give you the details,' she said, taking an A5 flyer from the pile on the side of the counter and pausing to write something on the back of it.

'Thanks,' Oliver said, folding the flyer up and putting it in his back pocket. He collected the coffees and found his way to a vacant seat and waited for Erin. It was turning into a really good day!

Chapter 21

ZARA

It was the Sunday of the bank holiday weekend and Zara was at a loose end. So far she'd managed to fill Saturday by going for a run, doing some grocery shopping, watching Netflix, and varnishing her toenails. Having me-time was a good thing, she told herself, but the four walls were beginning to close in on her. In the end she'd messaged Marsha from the gym to see if she wanted to hang out but she'd gone away with a friend to the Lake District. All her other girlfriends were in couples.

What she really wanted to do was go round to Amanda's and have a good old bitch about 'the Erin and Oliver situation'. But Amanda was in that blissful state of the newly married, and Zara didn't want to ruin her vibe just because she was sad, alone and single.

Erin was noticeably absent from the flat, no doubt at Oliver's. Zara had tried, and failed, not to imagine them at a cafe holding hands over cappuccinos with love heart foam or at the Tate gazing at some ridiculous modern artwork, with Oliver making his famous quips. So when Erin bounced into the kitchen with her carry bag that morning with a glow on, having obviously spent the night at his flat, it was hard not to imagine what they'd got up to there too.

Erin greeted her happily and sang a show tune under her breath as she knelt and bundled her dirty clothes into the washing machine. Zara, sitting at the table having a late breakfast of smashed avocado on toast, gritted her teeth. How did Oliver put up with the constant singing? Or maybe he liked musicals too. God, perhaps he did; she'd dodged a bullet there. She tried to make herself feel relief but all she felt was jealous.

Erin stood up and pressed the start button. 'There! I had to pop back as I was running out of clean clothes. I could wash them at Oliver's I suppose but he only has one drying rack and he just did a load,' she said conversationally.

'Ah,' replied Zara non-committedly. She didn't really want to get into a discussion about Oliver and clothes. Especially after the Sports Direct shopping excursion. In her mind's eye, she could still see Natasha fawning over him in his tight t-shirt and small shorts.

'We're going to the Columbia Road Flower Market this morning to get some plants for his balcony. He's interested in urban gardening,' Erin continued in a rush as if she had to tell someone.

Zara silently took a bite of her avocado toast, irked. That sounded fun. She'd like to do that.

'What are you up to today?' Erin asked, pouring cereal into a bowl.

'Nothing much. I thought I might go and do something. But I wasn't sure what,' said Zara, half hoping for an invite to go with them even though she knew it was a bad idea.

Erin must've thought so too because it wasn't forthcoming. Lala padded in, providing a welcome distraction so she didn't have to answer. 'Hello, my furry friend!' said Erin, bending down to pick her up. She staggered slightly under the cat's hefty weight and deposited her on the kitchen floor again in a hurry. Zara eyed them suspiciously, noting the way Lala was looking up at Erin in an expectant manner. 'You haven't been feeding her treats, have you?'

'No,' said Erin swiftly. 'Absolutely not. Well, I'd best get on. I'm meeting Oliver at eleven. Have fun whatever you get up to. It's a lovely day out there.'

'I will,' replied Zara. *All alone in single hell.*

Around lunchtime she had a text from her mum, inviting her over for dinner and the request: *Wear something colourful to celebrate summer!* Though Zara couldn't see much to celebrate about it. She really had to pull herself together and get over this whole Oliver–Erin thing. Maybe it was time she moved out to distance herself. But the thought of trying to find another flat made her shudder. It had taken long enough to find this one, and everything had been good up until now.

After rifling through her wardrobe to find something suitably summery, she settled on a pink top and a pair of green jeans she'd worn once.

'Oh, how lovely!' commented Kate when she opened the door, 'You look like a tulip.'

Zara grunted and handed her a Waitrose shopping bag containing snacks and drinks, her contribution to the meal.

Kate noted her grumpy expression but didn't say anything, gently shepherding her into the kitchen. Seated at the table were June and a man busily chopping vegetables.

'Hi,' said Zara, taken aback by the large mound of courgettes, carrots, asparagus and baby corn. She gathered whatever they were having for dinner was vegetable heavy. Which was fine by her. She'd slipped into a diet of fast food and heat-and-eat meals lately because she couldn't be bothered cooking.

'Hi, Zara.' June got up from the table and gave her a hug and a kiss on the cheek. 'This is my boyfriend, Gordon.'

'Hello, Gordon,' said Zara politely.

Gordon gave her a nod and a shy smile. Zara looked at

him curiously. She'd heard a lot about this internet dating conquest but never actually met him. In his early sixties, Gordon had a good head of grey hair that was closely cropped, a neatly trimmed silver goatee and a silver ring through one earlobe. He seemed quite trendy for an older guy. She liked his outfit, a purple satin waistcoat over a crisp white shirt.

'Take a seat. Gordon's cooking,' Kate told her. 'He's a Veggie. So we're accommodating him. Sorry if you were expecting a roast.'

'Ah. I was actually ...'

'I promise it's not too boring,' said Gordon good-naturedly, busy with his knife. 'There'll be plenty of herbs and spices in this concoction to give it some zing.'

'No, no, it sounds good. I need a vitamin boost anyway.'

'You are looking a little peaky, dear,' Kate said in a concerned tone, peering at her daughter's pale face. 'Let me make you a ginseng tea. Is it a bad time of the month?'

'I'm fine, Mum!' Zara said rather sharply, not wanting to discuss her periods in front of Gordon.

'It's alright, he's a gynaecologist,' piped up June. 'He's an expert on women's bits, aren't you, love?'

Gordon sighed and winked at Zara. 'I'm off duty.'

She relaxed a little. Well, if he was a *doctor* ... Though how June had managed to nab herself a trendy doctor on an internet dating site, she had no clue. Maybe there was hope for her after all.

She joined them at the table and popped a piece of carrot in her mouth. 'So what's the name of this internet dating site you met on?'

Chapter 22

OLIVER

Oliver couldn't afford PT sessions with Zara more than three times a week, but he had been going to the gym on the other days as well. He was definitely seeing the results, but it was a lot of work. A few of the regulars raised an eyebrow or nodded in greeting now when he walked in. That also extended to the staff. They didn't greet him by name or anything, there were far too many customers for that, but he was certainly on good terms with them. It was a good feeling to feel like you belonged rather than being a walking health and safety liability.

One particular day he was just moving the bench press machine so it was on an incline when he heard a voice behind him.

'Excuse me, could you possibly help me?'

He turned and almost yelped. She was tall and blonde and impeccably made up. She was wearing a white leotard over white tights, which did a magnificent job of showing off a very gym-toned body. 'I can't figure out how to get the right weights on this thing. Could you show me?'

Oliver smiled and followed her to the machine. It was one specifically for the legs, and he explained how to adjust the weights to how much she needed. She got herself settled, lying on her front with a leg under the rest. He was about to get back to his own exercises when she called out.

'Oh, would you be able to spot me? I usually run out of puff on the seventh or eighth rep.'

He looked around and one of the gym staff just happened to be walking by. Pete apparently, according to his name badge.

'Oh, Pete can help you if you like? Pete, would you be able to spot her?'

Pete grinned expansively and allowed that he might be able to be of assistance, giving Oliver a thumbs-up and mouthing a 'thank you' as he walked over to provide some hands-on guidance. Oliver managed to get back to his machine without someone muscling in on it.

On the way home, he stopped off at the street market for some vegetables. He really didn't get it, the market had little carts with all the vegetables on display, but they set up in the forecourt just in front of the supermarket. So in direct competition with the big chain store! How did they get away with that? And they charged more. The veg looked better though. The girl behind the cart smiled as he approached.

'Howdy, stranger! Haven't seen you for a bit; have you been avoiding me?'

Oliver smiled back. 'Never! Those potatoes are huge. Can I get two of those and a couple of those small onions?'

'Anything else?'

'No, that's shallot.'

He handed over his money as the realisation of his admittedly pretty poor pun registered on the girl's face. She laughed maybe a little too much, but he reveled in the feeling of someone getting his joke.

At work the next day, he was walking back from lunch, and for once the lift was working, so he decided to use that instead of going up the stairs. There were two of the marketing leads already in the lift when he got in, and one of them held the lift doors for him.

'Thanks!'

'No problem. You're on three, aren't you?'

'Yeah, I am.'

'You're one of the technical team, right? I'm having trouble with my computer and the projector in the large meeting room. Would you be able to come up to five to help me out?'

The lift stopped at two, and Sam got on, smiling a hello to Oliver. He smiled back before answering the marketing lead.

'Sure, I can pop up, no problem.' Out of the corner of his eye, he noticed that Sam was frowning. They both got out on three and headed to their respective desks. It didn't take long before Sam popped over to his desk for a chat.

'Hey, what was that all about in the lift?'

'The marketing ladies? They were having some issues with the projector and wanted some help.'

'Shouldn't they have called Lionel? He handles all the IT issues. Are you trying to muscle in on his turf?'

Oliver shook his head in confusion. 'No, I was just trying to be helpful. It was a bit strange that she asked me though. You know what those marketing folk are like; she probably just thought all us computer people deal with everything.'

Sam didn't say anything for a while, just looked at him, obviously taking her time to construct her sentences in her head. 'Olly, I despair, I really do. You're still with Erin, right?'

Oliver nodded slowly, not really seeing where she was coming from.

'OK, listen closely. The issue is that you're leading on all these women. They're looking for the slightest bit of encouragement, an inkling that you're available and possibly interested. And it's mean because although you're hot, you're also very taken. Unless you tell them that upfront, you're going to lead them on, and then they're going to be hurt when you finally let them down, or else they're going to be confused because you're giving them mixed signals, and that's arguably even worse. Are you listening to me?'

Oliver was staring into the mid-distance, replaying what she had just said in his head. 'Yeah ... yeah, thanks, Sam.'

Sam gave him a last look and seemed to be about to say something else but thought better of it and turned on her heel to head back to her desk.

Oliver sat staring after her, the conversation replaying over and over in his head and sticking on one phrase.

'Am I hot?' he asked himself.

Chapter 23

ZARA

Seeing how happy June was with Gordon inspired Zara to set her sights on an older man. It made a lot of sense. As June said, 'Forget boys in their thirties, they're still in nappies, love. Go for someone at least forty, they've got their shit together.'

With June's words ringing in her ears, she'd gone home and set up her profile on the internet dating site in question. Instead of choosing the thirty to thirty-five age band, she'd chosen forty to forty-five. This was new for her. She'd only ever dated guys around thirty, her own age. That's probably where she'd been going wrong. It was a revelation.

Almost immediately she started getting requests for dates which boosted her resolve even further. Now she didn't have to sit around wondering what Erin and Oliver were up to, she was getting a love life of her own.

The first guy who asked her out was Timothy, forty-two,

whom she met at the pub down the road. He bought her a drink and they chatted about movies and their respective jobs. But he didn't really have a sense of humour. She'd gotten used to Oliver telling her funny stories and making her laugh, so he paled by comparison. It was an easy 'no thanks' to a second drink and also to another date when he messaged her later that night. Zara updated her profile to make it clear that she liked funny guys.

The next date was a coffee with Daniel, forty, who fancied himself as a stand-up comedian. So she was forced to chuckle politely as he tried to impress her with his repertoire of bad jokes. It made her miss Oliver even more. He didn't have to *try*; he was just naturally funny. She declined a second date with Daniel.

The third date Zara had was with Lachlan, again at the pub. He was Irish, forty-three and starting to grey around the temples. His face was craggy like he'd spent the last decade partying hard and smoking a pack a day, so she was surprised to find out that he was into fitness. He lifted weights and went for ten-mile runs. Not only that, he was witty and knew how to hold a conversation. By the second drink, she warmed up to him considerably. Then it came out that he had a teenage son and an ex-wife. But he was open about it and she supposed that older men, even if they had their shit together, came with baggage. She accepted a second date with Lachlan, this time for dinner.

When she arrived at the gym for her lunchtime session with Oliver the next day, Zara was surprised to see him talking to a lithe brunette at the water fountain beside the stretching area. Weird. He never normally spoke to any women at the gym apart from her, and from their casual body language, she got the sense that they knew each other. She didn't get the chance to be introduced, though, because as she approached, the woman strolled off to the changing rooms. It was on the tip of Zara's tongue to ask him, 'Who's that?' but she was attempting to keep her distance from any kind of involvement in Oliver's personal life. Plus, she didn't want to come across as a busybody.

'Hi, are you ready?' she asked him.

'Hey. Yeah. Let's do it!'

They went through their usual warm-up routine, Zara starting with some standing stretches for quads and Oliver doing the same on an adjoining mat.

'How's your ankle after the physio?' he enquired.

'Yeah, good, thanks. I had a couple of sessions, and it's a lot better.'

Oliver nodded. She sensed he wanted to make a quip about her falling out of the tree. But he didn't, just commented, 'Nice day today.'

'Yes, let's hope the sun lasts until the weekend,' Zara replied.

Since he'd gotten together with Erin, the weather seemed to be the only thing of substance they chatted about these days. She sighed inwardly and moved into a downward dog, designed to lengthen the back and stretch the hamstrings.

Oliver had initially struggled with this pose, having virtually no flexibility in his hips. As she recalled, the first time he'd collapsed on the mat after ten seconds, gasping, saying it was 'too hard'. But she noticed, with a side-eye swivel, that he was now able to do it perfectly, even with the correct breathing as she'd taught him. It was quite impressive how far he'd come since his first session. Her gaze travelled over his lean body as he held the pose, evaluating him. There was hardly a quiver in his toned arm and thigh muscles, and he even had his legs straight and feet flat on the floor.

'Well done,' she said, unable to stop a note of admiration creeping into her voice. 'You've been practising that.'

'Maybe.' She couldn't see his face but could tell by his tone he was smiling.

He broke the pose and came down into a plank. As he did so, the movement caused something to fall out of his pocket and land in her range of vision. Still in her downward dog, Zara glanced at it. It looked like a flyer that had been folded in half. Oliver hadn't noticed, so she reached over with one hand and picked it up with the intention of giving it back to him. But it flipped open, and she saw it was for a band that had played at one of the local venues last month. On the corner was a scrawled mobile number in purple vivid and: *Text me if you go :-) Bianca xx.*

Zara came out of the pose and sat back on her heels, staring at the flyer, feeling uneasy. Why did he have this in his pocket?

'Did you see a band?' she remarked, handing it over when they were both standing up.

'Oh! Thanks. Yeah, I was thinking about it, but I didn't go.'

Zara couldn't help herself. 'What's with the phone number? And who's Bianca?'

Oliver shrugged. 'I don't know. Some girl gave it to me at a cafe ... I didn't ask for it,' he added.

'Does this happen a lot?'

'Yeah. I'm starting to get a little collection of numbers. Guess they all want the Olly monster.' He grinned at her, flexing a bicep.

Zara didn't smile back. A conversation she'd had with Erin the other day flashed into her mind. Zara had noticed she was unusually quiet and asked her what was wrong. Erin had mumbled something about Oliver being difficult to pin down lately and that he was never serious. Zara hadn't wanted to get into it, so she'd said something vague like, 'That's just his personality. He likes making jokes.'

But what Erin had said was now starting to make more sense. Was Oliver playing around? She didn't want to believe that of him, but why did he have the flyer in his pocket? Was he planning on messaging the girl?

She finished up their routine with some neck stretches, trying to figure out what to say. Or if she should say anything at all. She'd just decided to leave it well alone when the attractive brunette who Oliver had been talking with beforehand poked her head into the room. She was now dressed in office attire, hair scooped up in a sleek bun and her make-up carefully applied.

'Hey, Olly. See you at the usual after work?'

Oliver looked guiltily at Zara. 'Maybe not this time.'

The woman shrugged. 'Suit yourself,' she said and exited through the glass sliding doors.

After she was well out of earshot, Zara rounded on Oliver. 'What was that about?'

'Nothing.'

'It didn't sound like nothing. Why are you meeting strange women at the pub?'

'She's not strange. She's Holly,' said Oliver, trying to make a joke, but Zara wasn't in the mood for his quips. She narrowed her eyes at him.

Oliver held up his hands. 'Hey, I'm not doing anything wrong. I'm just being friendly.'

'It looks *too* friendly. Are you cheating on Erin?'

Oliver looked taken aback. 'What?'

'You heard me.' Zara put her hands on her hips. 'You've got a flyer in your pocket with a woman's number on it that you *didn't* chuck out, and now it turns out you've been meeting another one at the pub! No wonder Erin's paranoid. Looks like she's got good reason to be.'

'Now hang on a second ...' said Oliver tersely. 'Just because a few women have shown me attention, it doesn't mean I'm cheating on my girlfriend. Why shouldn't I have friends who are girls?'

'Oliver, I'm just saying what I'm seeing ... and what I'm seeing doesn't look good from where I'm standing.'

'Maybe you're just jealous I'm getting attention,' Oliver shot back. 'Yeah, that's more like it.'

Zara laughed nervously. 'Jealous? Yeah right. That's *not* what this is about.'

'I think it is. When I was overweight, I never had women give me the time of day, now I'm fit and they are, you're trying to rain on my parade.'

'I'm not trying to rain on anything. But you're going out with my flatmate, and I don't particularly want to know that you're having drinks with other women at the pub and shit.'

'That's easily fixed. If you can't handle me having a social life, maybe we shouldn't train together any more,' Oliver retorted.

'That suits me just fine! As of now, I'm no longer your PT,' Zara snapped, sick of his cocky attitude.

Oliver's eyes widened as if he hadn't really expected her to agree. Then he turned and walked as quickly as he could over the squashy mats like he couldn't get away from her fast enough.

Chapter 24

OLIVER

Life at the gym without Zara wasn't too bad. He had been training with her for so long that he was on autopilot, which was good. He didn't even think about it, he just blinked and he was at the gym's front door with his gym gear and trainers on.

Where he noticed her absence was all the other times. The stretches: he had to do those from memory rather than copying her on the mat beside him. The weights: now he had to actually memorise them on each of the machines. She didn't even have to write any of that stuff down, and he knew that she had a whole bunch of other clients, so it's not like she was just remembering just his stats. And she also remembered his performance from the previous sessions and when it was the right time to increase the weights. Plus having her on the treadmill beside him was almost a comfort. Having someone sharing the pain made it more bearable.

He raised the incline of the treadmill a little more, hearing the whine of the motor, which raised the running platform over the steady *plod plod* of his feet and the whir of the mat whizzing along. The extra angle changed which muscles were being worked, and he started to sweat even more. He couldn't get her words out of his head though, and he couldn't figure out why. When Sam had had a go at him at work, it was like water off a duck's back. Except that bit about being hot. He liked that. But he wasn't leading anyone on; they just hadn't asked him if he had a girlfriend. If they had, he would have told them, so it really wasn't his fault.

And if random girls gave him their number, well, there was no harm in hanging onto those messages, was there? They made him happy. It was nice to be liked. And again, it wasn't like he was sleeping with anyone else. Although Holly from the gym had looked disappointed that time he'd met her for a drink at the bar after the gym and then headed home at about ten. Almost like she'd been slapped, if he was honest. Maybe he had given her the wrong idea?

The more he thought about it (leg muscles starting to really work now), the more he realised that what irked him most was the fact that Zara had an unflattering opinion of him. That's what really hurt. Not that he had done anything wrong. Because he hadn't ... right?

The day at work limped along slowly. He still went up and down the stairs two at a time and measured his recovery time in seconds, but the bounce had gone out of his step. He didn't want to talk about Zara with Sam as he already knew where she stood on the matter. Toby on the other hand may have a unique perspective. He didn't have to wait too long to have the opportunity for a chat about the subject; he bumped into him at the kitchenette, making a cup of coffee. Oliver didn't bother with the coffee machines as they were the professional ones: an effort at employee benefits by their employer. It had the unfortunate effect of cutting coffee from Oliver's diet as he had no idea how they worked, even after being shown twice. He guessed he should have been paying more attention to what the Italian barista had been doing behind the counter rather than what she was writing on the back of the flyer.

'Was that you I saw in the Hat and Tun last week?' asked Toby as he banged the little metal thingy against the rubbish bin, the coffee grounds falling into the bin.

'Maybe. I go there occasionally.'

'Was that your girlfriend that you were with? She was hot!'

'Uh, no … that was Holly. She's just a friend.'

Toby gave an appreciative head nod. 'Looking to trade up already … nice! Well, I won't tell anyone. She looked into you anyway!'

'Oh no, it's not like that at all.'

Toby frowned. 'Does this Holly know that you have a girlfriend? She was laser locked on you! I wish the girls I went out with looked at me like that!'

Oliver shook his head. He was about to explain that it hadn't come up in conversation and that he wasn't hiding the fact, and that he hadn't thought it important enough to mention when Toby continued. 'Nice! Definitely don't tell her. And don't tell your girlfriend about her either! If you play your cards right, you'll be able to keep them both on the go at the same time! There's always room for another side chick!'

Oliver half smiled, half grimaced. And wished this conversation was over. Well, now he was sure of it; if Toby approved of a course of action, then it was definitely the wrong one! Which meant that, of course, he had to unpick all the coffees and drinks that he'd been having and review all the accompanying conversations to see if he had been saying anything which could be misread. Aw, man, Sam was right. And he'd been wrong.

Chapter 25

ZARA

Zara had so far successfully managed to avoid any interaction with Oliver. She'd seen him a few times at the gym working out solo, but only from a distance. Other PTs would probably see it as a natural end to their contract and say, 'Ah, well, you'll get over it—shit happens. There are plenty more clients out there …' But to her, their blow-up wasn't a small thing. Oliver wasn't just a client; he was a friend. And there didn't seem to be any way back from their disagreement. Apart from her apologising, of course, but she couldn't bring herself to do that because part of her felt she was in the right.

Every time she thought of his grin and 'they all want the Olly monster' comment she got angry again. He'd turned into a dick. She'd seen this happen before. Perfectly nice guys had their egos inflated when they trimmed down and gained a muscle or two. The female attention after years of neglect was like a dopamine hit and they went all silly. Though, as she'd reluctantly admitted to herself, it didn't mean he *was* cheating on Erin. Even if it looked that way. She had no actual proof of that, and it had been unfair of her to accuse him of it. The turning into a dick part, yes; the cheating part, no.

She hadn't told Erin about no longer being his PT because she'd most likely ask awkward questions, so she left it well alone. One evening a few weeks later, she was in the kitchen making a salmon, avocado and chickpea salad when Erin breezed in.

'I've just booked the table at Saucy Mama's!' she announced.

Zara looked at her blankly.

'For my thirtieth birthday. It's on the eighteenth—you said you'd come, remember?' Erin frowned at her.

Shit. Zara had completely forgotten she'd promised to go to the Italian restaurant.

'Yes, of course. How many people are going again?' she enquired hesitantly.

'Eight—four friends from work, plus you, me and Oliver, and Lachlan, of course, if he wants to come.'

Zara relaxed. So not too intimate, and she could bring a date. If she got there early, she could wangle it so she was sitting at the other end of the table from Oliver so she didn't have to speak to him. Then, looking at her flatmate's now smiling face, she felt guilty that she hadn't sorted it out. Erin was bound to notice the frosty atmosphere, and she shouldn't have to play go-between on her birthday. Maybe she should come clean.

'Erin, there's something I have to tell you. Me and Oliver aren't …'

'Yes, yes, I know.' Erin flapped a hand, brushing her words aside. 'You're not his PT anymore. He told me.'

Zara paused in her salad tossing. 'Oh, what did he say?'

'Just that he was at a stage where he felt good about himself and that he was focusing on maintenance. But he said to tell you that he appreciates your hard work because he was a difficult case, whatever that means.'

Zara breathed out. So Oliver had done the right thing and told Erin they weren't training together. That was nice of him. And he'd managed to compliment her PT abilities in a roundabout way. Zara partially thawed towards him. Perhaps he wasn't that much of a dick.

'What time have you booked the table for? I'll put it in my calendar now,' she told Erin, mentally making a note to go shopping for a present. Something really nice to make up for being angry at her boyfriend.

She mentioned the birthday dinner to Lachlan the next time she saw him. They were still mostly on midweek pub dates, apart from having been out for dinner once. A Japanese bistro in Acton, where he lived. Living nearby was a tick in his favour. About everything else to do with Lachlan, Zara was on the fence. He was a nice guy in general and seemed interested in her from what she could gather. But she wasn't sure whether she really wanted to be in a relationship with him. It was nothing tangible. She just didn't think she could grow to like him more than she already did. If he messaged to say he'd met someone else, she had a feeling she wouldn't give two hoots. Anyway, he was keen to go to the dinner, which was a relief. Turning up alone would be worse than having to make conversation with Oliver.

As it was, on the night of the dinner, Zara found herself taking particular care over what she wore, a sapphire-blue silk dress she'd bought for the occasion. She even got out her curling irons to give her dead-straight hair some bounce. It was for Lachlan, she told herself, ignoring her jerky heartbeat whenever she thought about being near Oliver. There were other people going, so it was unlikely they'd even exchange one single word. A mere nod. That's all she was expecting from him.

The restaurant was in Ealing Broadway, so Zara ordered an Uber, not wanting to walk through Walpole Park in heels. Lachlan met her outside the entrance wearing his battered brown leather jacket, a black shirt and jeans. He looked ruggedly handsome, if not quite as presentable as she would've liked as it was normally what he wore to the pub. *Stop it, Zara, you're being picky,* she told herself, *no one's going to care!*

Inside the restaurant, there was a general atmosphere of bustle; it was busy even for midweek, Zara noted. Saucy Mama's was relatively new in town with bright, modern decor, hanging baskets and a living wall of fragrant herbs. Erin loved her potted plants, so it wasn't surprising she wanted to come here.

They waited at the entrance until a passing server noticed them. 'Hi, have you got a reservation?'

'Yes, for 7pm, under the name of Erin.'

'Oh, yes, follow me, please,' said the server. They were led to two tables set for four that had been pushed together opposite a long plush banquette. Zara and Lachlan were the first to arrive, she saw, even though it was well after seven. Where was Erin?

'I don't think this is right,' she told the server. 'It's meant to be for eight people.'

He frowned. 'Nooo? The table for Erin is definitely just four.'

Zara sat on the banquette with Lachlan next to her. Where the fuck was everyone? She took out her phone to see if she had any messages. Nothing. Erin was coming from work with her friends, so she must be driving everyone in.

She was just about to ring her when Erin turned up, carrying a large bouquet of yellow roses. 'Sorry, I got held up in a meeting!' She plonked the flowers on the banquette next to Zara.

'That's OK,' said Zara, relieved to see her. She got up to give her a hug. 'Happy birthday!'

'Happy birthday,' Lachlan echoed, also getting up to give her a kiss on the cheek. 'Are we expecting anyone else?'

'Yeah, just Oliver. The others bailed,' said Erin sitting in the chair opposite Lachlan. 'Hence the flowers. But they've all got kids, and you know how it is, family first.'

Zara's blood turned icy. 'But it's your thirtieth? Couldn't they get babysitters?'

Erin shrugged. 'Apparently not. So it's great you guys came! Otherwise, I'd be sitting here all by myself. Boo hoo me.'

'Where's Oliver?'

'He's on his way.'

The server poured them water from a glass jug. 'I'll be back for your drinks order,' he sang and went off again. Zara shook her head. It was just the four of them. A fricken double date! There was no hiding at the end of the table. She gazed at the empty chair directly in front of her. Oliver was going to be sitting right there! She felt trapped and had a sudden urge to flee.

Erin was talking to Lachlan, and she forced herself to listen while glancing nervously at the entrance. Oliver was going to walk through the door any minute.

Chapter 26

OLIVER

Oliver made his way to Saucy Mama's from the train station. Ealing Broadway was a long way from Central London, so he had decided to meet Erin at the restaurant rather than try and connect with her in the city, just in case there were any delays. He'd been lucky there weren't, though it had still taken the better part of an hour to get there. It always helped to have a couple of options in terms of underground lines.

He hurried past the shops, cafes and restaurants, glancing from time to time at his phone with the map before catching a glimpse of Erin through the plate-glass windows of the restaurant in question. The server at the door looked up with a smile as he entered and nodded as he indicated that he was joining an already seated party.

The other two seats were taken with Zara and an older guy. He gave Erin a hug, said hi to Zara and introduced himself to the new guy.

'Hi, I'm Oliver,' he said, holding out his hand.

The guy was well put together, if maybe ten years older than the others at the table. 'I'm Lachlan,' he said warmly. Oliver focused all his attention on Lachlan. Mainly because Zara was wearing a silk dress which perfectly matched her eyes, and the fabric clung to a body honed by years in the gym. Gawping at her in front of Erin would be the exact thing that Zara had accused him of doing, so he had to prove that he wasn't like that.

The server swooped in with menus, pausing to let them know that the specials were Linguine alle Vongole and Grilled Sea Bass with Lemon Caper Sauce before taking their drink orders. Zara ordered a double gin and tonic, which was out of character for her—Oliver didn't think that he had ever seen her on the spirits, so he guessed she was a little nervous about tonight. Well, Oliver would try and make it less awkward if he could.

'So, how did you two meet?' he asked Lachlan.

Lachlan smiled. 'We met online, actually. Zara is a lot more age appropriate for me.'

Oliver didn't know how to interpret that. 'Have you been going out for very long?'

'Oh, just a few weeks. It takes a special woman to get me off the market. Quite a lot of disappointed ladies out there, I tell you! You know how it is, right, Oliver?'

Oliver's answering smile didn't quite reach his eyes. Lachlan's response set the scene for the rest of the evening. Oliver could have interpreted it as an attempt to connect with him, but it came across as if Lachlan was seeking approval for a particular type of behaviour, and as the evening progressed, that behaviour became more and more apparent. After they had ordered their food, they decided to give the presents. Zara gave Erin a Jo Malone candle which was enthused over. And then Oliver got out his present. It was in a long box, the type in which you would normally get a necklace from a jeweller. Erin's eyes lit up. Oliver realised too late that the box shape and size had set her expectations. Oh no, this could go badly, he thought.

Erin opened the box, pulling out two A4 pieces of paper which had been folded three times. Oliver could almost see the giant question mark over her head as she tried to process what it was. Zara exclaimed, 'Read it, read it!'

Erin took the first of the pieces of paper. 'Ah, let's see. This is a hotel booking confirmation ... for the Hotel dell'Arte ... which is in ... Venice. And for that weekend that we were talking about. Ah ... OK, and the other one? That's flights to Venice for that weekend too.'

Oliver grimaced internally. Her reaction to the candle was so much more genuine and excited. And his weekend in Venice was obviously nowhere as well received. He couldn't figure it out. Was it because it was Italy? He had made sure that she had nothing else on that weekend and that she hadn't already been to Venice. But maybe that was because she had never wanted to go there.

He was saved from any further discussion of Erin's disappointment by the arrival of their waiter bearing their starters. They talked of other things over the food, and then Lachlan excused himself and made his way to the bathrooms. 'He seems nice,' he said to Zara. She smiled politely but didn't say anything, which was a little unnerving. He tried a change of subject, but that didn't seem to be working either, so Oliver excused himself and headed in the same direction as Lachlan.

The bathrooms were in the basement, and Oliver bumped into Lachlan as he was leaving to make his way back to the girls. He was rubbing his nose and sniffling and didn't seem to see Oliver as they passed in the corridor. Oliver was shaking his head and trying to figure that out when he entered the bathroom. There was someone washing their hands angrily in the sink.

'You alright, mate?' Oliver asked.

'Fucking druggies, man. If it's not the junkies shooting up in the cubicles, it's the posh twats with their Colombian marching powder.'

Oliver looked at him blankly.

'Cocaine, man.'

The penny dropped. He pointed at the door. 'That guy? He was doing blow?'

The other guy plucked a paper towel from the dispenser. 'Yup, had the nerve to offer me some too. I sent him packing.'

'Huh, at least he was sharing! Well, have a good night.'

'Yeah, you too.'

Well, this was awkward. Did he tell Zara or not? Would she see it as some sort of retaliation for telling him off for his bad behaviour? Would it be him meddling with her relationship? Aw, man.

Oliver headed back up and returned to his seat. While he had been away, there had been an addition to the seat beside them. A couple sat there, the lady on the banquette along the wall beside Lachlan. She was a sight, an evening dress with a plunging neckline and cleavage which could have swallowed a car. The guy she was with was tall, balding, with a comb-over and a good fifteen years older than her. They seemed to be getting along nicely enough though.

It wasn't long before their food was delivered; Oliver's steak was cooked to perfection, with a bearnaise sauce and a selection of miniature roasted vegetables as a nod to balance. They were all tucking in with gusto when there was a clatter from the table next door. Apparently the lady of the pair had dropped her fork from the starter and was leaning down to collect it. Lachlan's eyes were practically bulging out of their sockets as he enjoyed a privileged front-row seat. He turned to make contact with Oliver and indicated where the show was with his eyebrows and subtle eye gestures. The lady in the seat next door seemed to have trouble finding the fork, and Lachlan's gestures became more and more pronounced as Oliver continued to ignore them. Erin and Zara were right there, for God's sake! He made a point of carefully considering every bite of his steak, eventually leaning over and asking Erin and Zara about their meals. With a shuffling of seats, the cutlery conundrum was resolved next door, and the twitching from Lachlan subsided.

Ten minutes later, they had all finished their mains, and the waiter had replenished their drinks, dropping off the dessert menus. 'It wouldn't hurt to have a look …' quipped Oliver.

Chapter 27

ZARA

Zara couldn't believe Erin had been so dismissive of Oliver's thoughtful gift. A trip to Venice! That was amazing. She had to physically stop herself from exclaiming, 'I'll go if she doesn't want to!' Strangely she got a vivid image of her and Oliver strolling along beside a canal in the late afternoon sunlight licking ice cream cones. It was a pleasant image, and she contemplated it for a little while, imagining what they might talk about.

'Zara, are you going to have dessert?' Erin's voice filtered through and she came back to reality. Everyone was looking at her, including the server.

'Oh, er, I'm not sure?' She looked around but there didn't seem to be menus. Oh, there they were under the server's arm, he must've collected them while she was tuned out. She saw Oliver gazing at her and flushed.

'I'm getting the sorbet,' he said quietly.

'What flavour?'

'Lemon.'

'I'll have one of those,' she said to the server, who nodded and scurried off.

'Very healthy, you two,' commented Erin. 'Was this part of the original diet plan?'

'Oh, he didn't have a diet plan,' said Zara. 'I'm not really a stickler for that.'

'What's this?' asked Lachlan.

'Didn't she tell you? Zara was Oliver's personal trainer. I don't know what he looked like before she put him through his paces, but the after version is fantastic.' She squeezed Oliver's bicep, and he looked uncomfortable.

'I wanted to get fit for travel and I'd put on a bit of weight during Covid,' he explained to Lachlan. 'It was never about having a certain look though. Zara understood that. She was really encouraging too.'

Oliver shifted his eyes to Zara pensively. Was he worried she might mention how women were throwing themselves at him, and he wasn't doing much to dissuade them? What did he take her for? She wasn't going to get into *that* on Erin's birthday.

'You put the work in. I just provided the guidance,' she said evenly, avoiding his eyes.

'Can't hurt that you got a girlfriend at the end of it

though,' Lachlan remarked. 'Good on you, mate. You make a great couple.'

Zara couldn't believe it. Was Lachlan actually at the same dinner she was? The man had the sensitivity of a walrus. There was obviously tension between Oliver and Erin over the whole Venice thing. The look on his face when Erin had folded the pieces of paper and put them in the box without a word was a mixture of hurt and confusion. She didn't blame him. She would be too if she were in his position.

Oliver changed the subject and mentioned that he'd started training for the Richmond half marathon. Lachlan said he'd done it and that it was a scenic route.

'Great,' said Erin, pouting. 'So I guess I'm not going to see you much then?'

'You could always train with me,' said Oliver.

Erin wrinkled her nose. 'Ugh, running. No thanks. I'd rather watch *Cats*, and that's my least favourite musical.'

Oliver said nothing and ate his sorbet in silence. Zara watched him feeling helpless. Wanting to reassure him that he could do it.

'I'm sure you'll do really well,' she said finally, trying to be encouraging.

'You think?' Oliver sounded unsure.

'Of course. You're very self-motivated. That was obvious during our sessions. Besides, setting fitness goals is always a good thing.'

'Thanks, yeah, I think so too. Especially now that I'm training on my own. I've downloaded an app to keep track of my running times.'

It actually sounded like fun, Zara thought. She could train with him. Not as a PT but as a friend. Maybe they could do the marathon together? She opened her mouth, feeling excited by the prospect, then promptly shut it again. He was Erin's boyfriend, not hers.

Zara was relieved when the dinner came to an end. What with Erin's work friends not turning up, her weird reaction to the Venice trip, and the tension between her and Oliver, her nerves were strung out. All she wanted to do was go home and relax with a chamomile tea.

But then outside the restaurant, Erin and Oliver grabbed an Uber back to his place, and she ended up stranded with Lachlan. She got out her phone to order one, but he beat her to it.

'We can share if you like?' he offered, with the app already open and actively searching for a nearby car.

'But you're in the opposite direction?' She saw too late how this was going to play out. They had been on at least half a dozen pub dates and now two dinners, so it wasn't strange that he should try and take it to the next level. And under normal circumstances, Zara may have been tempted.

But at the restaurant, sitting across from Oliver, Zara had been reminded of how much she liked him. Their disagreement now seemed petty. Especially in light of Lachlan's behaviour, which was so much worse. His comments about her being more 'age appropriate' for him and his ogling the woman's cleavage and trying to get Oliver to join in had highly embarrassed her. Why would he think she wouldn't see? She was right there! Oliver had redeemed himself in her eyes by ignoring him completely.

'That's fine. They can drop me off after you,' said Lachlan, tapping to confirm the pick-up point. 'I'll pay for both trips.'

'OK,' Zara agreed, thinking when they got to her flat she'd make a run for it.

But she misjudged how many beers Lachlan had drunk. As soon as the car took off his hand was on her knee, sliding upwards underneath the silk material. She batted it away. Two minutes later, he tried again.

'*Don't!*'

'I thought we were together?' he wheedled.

'We've been on a few dates, that's all. To see if we're suited,' Zara replied. 'At no point did we discuss being boyfriend and girlfriend.'

Lachlan sniggered. 'Boyfriend and girlfriend? This isn't *Grange Hill*.' He shifted closer, and she could smell the stench of beer fumes. 'What's say I save money on the Uber and just stay at yours?'

Here we go, Zara thought.

'Sorry, I've got to get up early for a workout,' she said sharply.

'We could have a workout of our own—tonight.' He waggled his eyebrows at her.

'I don't think so,' she muttered.

'Aw c'mon, don't be like that.' He pursed his wet lips and lurched toward her. She saw the slobbery kiss coming and turned her face at the last minute. He managed to smooch her cheek, leaving a wet lip imprint. She wiped it off with the back of her hand, feeling revulsed. Why did men always turn into idiots after a few too many beers? Wasn't he supposed to know better since he was more mature? Age didn't seem to come into it when alcohol was involved.

'I really like you, Zara. You're a cool gal,' Lachlan slurred.

Gal? Zara shuddered and tried to move as close to the door as possible, away from him. And his beery breath.

When they pulled up at her flat, she opened the car door immediately and got out with a 'Thanks!' to the driver. Zara sensed Lachlan moving behind her to follow and closed the door smartly, but it cracked him on the shin.

Lachlan cried out in pain and fell back on the seat, clutching it. 'Ow, ow, ow!' he shouted melodramatically.

'Oi, mate, are you coming or going?' asked the driver

impatiently, half turning with a frown. 'I've got another pick-up.'

'He's going to Acton,' said Zara firmly to the driver. 'Sorry about the leg, Lachlan. Best get home and ice it. If it comes up in a bruise, I recommend arnica gel.'

She slammed the car door and sprinted up the path feeling like she'd had a lucky escape.

Chapter 28

OLIVER

The more Oliver thought about Erin, the more he suspected that she wasn't the right one for him. He was positive that it wasn't because of her reaction to the Venice present, although that added to it, sure. But it wasn't just a knee-jerk reaction. They just had very little in common. Once he came to that conclusion, his next step became more obvious. Though he left off calling her until a week after the Saucy Mama's dinner. He didn't want to ruin her birthday mood.

'Hey, Erin, do you want to grab a coffee? I think we need to have a talk.'

'Great idea. I've been meaning to grab some time with you.'

They arranged the time and place for the next day. Which gave Oliver enough time to replay the conversation with her in his head. She had seemed upbeat, but his understanding of relationship code words made him think that he had pretty much put her on notice that he was going to break up with her. What else does 'I think we need to have a talk' mean? It could only really have one meaning, surely?

He was a couple of minutes early for their meeting and habitually ordered their coffees. It was a different cafe from their regular, and while the barista was friendly enough, Oliver didn't linger at the counter and found a table in the secluded corner. Erin was on time and gave him a hug hello.

'Thanks for coming,' Oliver started.

'Why wouldn't I? Anyway I wanted to talk about—'

'Let me go first—'

'No, I want to go first.' Oliver conceded with an 'after you' gesture.

She took a sip of her coffee and picked up a napkin and started to tear little bits off the edges. She stared at the table top intently before beginning. 'Oliver, I think we're in very different places in our lives. Look, I'm thinking babies and a house in the suburbs, and you're wasting your money living in the city and jetting all over Europe. I think I need to find someone who values the same things.' She didn't seem too upset by what she was saying, and although she was frowning, there was an iron resolve emanating from her.

Oliver nodded. 'I agree entirely,' he said.

'Don't try to persuade me otherwise. I mean, the sex is great, better than great. Obviously. But—Sorry? What?'

'I agree. I think we should break up.'

'Oh.' There was a pause while they considered the contents of their respective coffees.

Oliver was at a bit of a loss as to what to say next. 'Thank you for your time' seemed very professional. He settled for, 'It was fun. I hope you find what you're looking for. I really do.' That was a little cringe, but it sort of summed up where he was at. He was out of the habit of relationships and their own language. If it were up to him, he would have high-fived and said something cool like, 'Sorry it didn't work out, let's hope the next one is better for both of us, huh?' But that probably wouldn't be appreciated. The truth rarely was.

There was another couple of minutes of contemplative silence, staring into coffee cups. Oliver finished his and chased the last of the foam around the bottom of the mug with a spoon.

'Will you be able to get a refund on your flights?' Erin asked.

'Oh, I can get the name changed, and maybe I'll take one of the guys from work.'

'Ah, good. At least they won't go to waste.'

'Yeah. Hey, I have to go now. Uh ... but I'm serious. It was good, you know, while it lasted. But ... it's for the best.'

He got up. She stood up too, standing awkwardly. He gave her a hug and a peck on the cheek and walked toward the door. You'd think at the age of thirty-one this sort of thing would somehow get easier, he thought angrily as he opened the door. But it was just the same as when he was thirteen. He concentrated on the physical act of getting back to his flat as if everything was new to him. It helped that he had something to occupy his brain. Once he got home, he waited for the wave of grief or sadness or ... something, anything to hit him, but he felt nothing at all. He couldn't figure it out. Was he a heartless arsehole who felt nothing for the love of his life? OK, it had only been a couple of months. But still, did the fact that he felt nothing about the breakup mean that he had no feelings for Erin? That he should not have even gone out with her in the first place?

That was a conundrum that he didn't know whether he wanted to solve. There didn't seem to be an angle which didn't make him out to be a bastard. Either he had no feelings for her, in which case arguably he should never have been with her in the first place, or else he did have feelings for her and he was suppressing these.

Oliver decided that he couldn't be arsed cooking and would swap his Friday takeaway night for that night's tarragon and leek pork tenderloin. A brief visit to his favourite takeaway delivery site later, he was curled up on his couch with a bowl of Malaysian street food and a large glass of merlot, half watching a movie. He was still mulling over his lack of emotional response when he finally came to a conclusion. He had been giving himself a hard time for not having an emotional connection but that would have to have grown while they were together. The kind of connection that he had been seeking all his life wasn't always instant when you started to go out with someone. It grew in the right conditions, and if you gave it the right conditions and it wasn't growing, you could be generous and give it some more time, or else you could do what both he and Erin had done, which was to pull the plug on it.

Once he came to that conclusion, Oliver expected to be overcome with regret and maybe cry a bit. And he was *sad*, but he would have been sadder if Erin had not wanted to end it too, because he would have been feeling bad for her loss. But as it was, he just felt slightly down that they'd broken up, and he figured, after a good night's sleep, he'd be ready for the next chapter in his romantic life.

Chapter 29

ZARA

Lachlan hadn't messaged since the birthday dinner but that was fine with Zara. She had nothing to say to him. Anyway, she had her hands full with three new clients that had been referred to her. She wasn't sure, but she had a feeling Oliver had something to do with it. They'd all said the same thing, that it was a colleague at work who had recommended her. But then they hadn't wanted to name names when she'd asked who it was. Had he been giving out her details at his office and telling them not to say it was him?

Erin had taken a few days off work to stay with her parents in the Cotswolds, so Zara couldn't ask her about it. That was strange as well. She *never* visited them. But maybe she was playing the dutiful daughter. Being out of the loop and trying to figure out what was going on with other people was exhausting, so Zara was just trying to concentrate on her own life. And ignore Oliver. Not easy when they both went to the same gym.

The day after Erin arrived back, Zara was in the middle of a lunchtime session with a client when Oliver came running over to her with a panicked expression and his phone pressed to his ear. 'I'm with her now. I'll tell her unless you want to speak to her? OK, I'll put her on.'

Zara frowned at him. 'Oliver, I'm with a—'

'It's Erin, and it's about Lala. You probably want to take it.'

Zara grabbed his phone and moved away out of earshot of her client, who was looking at them curiously. 'Hi, Erin?'

'Sorry, I tried ringing, but you didn't pick up …'

'What's wrong?'

Erin drew a shaky breath. 'Lala's had some kind of episode. I found her lying on the kitchen floor when I got home from the supermarket. I wrapped her in a blanket and drove like mad to the vet in Ealing Broadway. I'm here with her now.'

Zara's legs went weak, and she leaned against one of the machines. 'Is she … she's not …?' She couldn't bring herself to say the word: *Dead*.

Out of the corner of her eye she saw Oliver had taken over as substitute PT and was counting the client's sit-ups in a businesslike manner.

'She was unconscious but alive. The vet is just running

some tests on her now. You might want to get here, though. She didn't look good. And, um, I kind of need to go to work. I've got a presentation. Otherwise I'd stay, sorry.'

'No, you go. I'll leave now. Thanks so much for taking her.'

'Message me when you know what the story is. I hope she's OK.'

Zara rang off, her head in a whirl. Her client was finishing up and doing some leg stretches with Oliver guiding him in what to do. Oliver caught her eye and mouthed, 'Are you OK?'

She shook her head.

'Right. That's it for this session,' he said meaningfully. 'Good job.'

Zara catapulted into action. 'Sorry about that Mr Grenfell. A family emergency,' she said. 'I'll see you Thursday?'

The client nodded and seemed happy enough, thanks to Oliver's quick thinking. He walked off to the changing room.

'Thanks for filling in. I need to go to the vet asap. As Erin probably told you.' She fought to keep the wobble out of her voice without much success.

'Do you want me to come with you? You look a bit pale,' said Oliver.

Zara wavered. Having company would be good.

'Don't you have to go to work?'

'Ah, they can do without me for one afternoon. It's a family emergency, after all.' He winked at her, and she smiled weakly. 'Let me call a black cab. Getting an Uber might be difficult this time of day.'

Something about Oliver's take-charge attitude was extremely reassuring. And in the cab, he sensed she just wanted to be left alone with her thoughts and didn't try to distract her with mindless chatter. It was just what she needed.

At the vet's, Zara steeled herself for the worst, but the receptionist was kind, telling them to take a seat in the waiting room and she'd find out what was happening. There was a poster of a kitten on the wall, and Zara felt herself getting emotional, thinking of when her mum had bought Lala for her eight years ago. She'd been going through a hard time after her dad died, and it was the best present Kate could have given her. Lala was so attention-seeking that she demanded Zara think about her rather than wallow.

She tried to look on the bright side. Lala wasn't that old, she was just overweight. And that didn't necessarily mean she had to be put down.

'What do you think happened?' asked Oliver.

Zara picked at the side of her fingernail. 'Any number of things. Lala isn't the world's healthiest cat. She's overweight.'

Oliver stared at her. '*You* have a fat cat?' The amazement on his face made her want to giggle. But this wasn't the time for laughing.

'I do,' she replied soberly. 'I feel so bad. I should've kept a closer eye on her. I tried putting her on a diet. But it obviously didn't work.'

'Wow. Sounds like you've got a new client. Do you think they build cat treadmills?'

Zara gave a small smile at the thought. 'I could get her some cat gym gear. I'm sure it's a thing. But she likes her food and she's pretty lazy. I'm going to have my work cut out for me.'

'Sounds like this cat and I might have quite a lot in common,' Oliver joked.

'It's been worse lately. Erin's been on a musicals binge and going through the Jammie Dodgers like no one's business, so I assume Lala's managed to get quite a few titbits. It's like she's comfort eating or something.'

Oliver looked guilty. 'Um, so I could be the reason for that.'

'Oh?' Zara had assumed her grouchiness was a bad bout of PMT.

'Yeah, things weren't going too well between us and then, of course, the break-up ...'

Zara sat up straighter in the plastic chair. 'What? She

never said anything. When?'

'Last week.'

'That explains the time off work and the visit to her parents. You're obviously still on speaking terms if she rang you at the gym though?'

Oliver shrugged. 'Yeah, it was a mutual thing, so maybe she doesn't hate my guts too much.'

'What happened?'

'Let's just say the Venice present was the beginning of the end. She's more interested in settling down, which I'm definitely not ready for. Anyway, long story short, I'm moving on. And I'm focusing on the half marathon.'

Zara wanted to ask more questions about the breakup, but she decided to stick with, 'How's the training going?'

'It's going. I'm struggling to make progress, to be honest. At this rate I'll be lucky if I manage five miles.'

'Well, I could—' Zara was interrupted by a slim Indian woman wearing a white lab coat coming into the waiting room.

'Zara? I'm Dr Joshi.'

'Yes, that's me.' Zara jumped up. 'How's Lala?'

The vet smiled at her anxious expression. 'She's awake now.' She glanced curiously at Oliver. 'This is Oliver, my friend,' Zara said and the vet nodded. 'Let's go through to my office and you can see her.'

'Thank you.'

Zara and Oliver followed the vet down a corridor and into an examining room. Lala was in a cat cage on a table. She gave a mew when she saw Zara. 'Can I pat her?'

'Of course.' Dr Joshi seated herself by her computer and tapped to bring up a browser.

'Hey, missy. I was so worried about you.' Zara opened the cage door, and Lala walked out nonchalantly onto the table as if to say, 'What's all the commotion?' Zara wanted to bury her face in her cat's fur and sob but she held back her tears, not wanting to embarrass herself in front of Oliver. She settled for stroking her fur.

'Hi, Lala.' Oliver gave her a wave, standing back a little, not wanting to intrude on the reunion.

'Sooo,' said Dr Joshi, 'the test has confirmed that Lala has Type II diabetes.'

'Diabetes!' said Zara. 'I thought only humans got that?'

'Not at all. It's very common in cats too. Especially Burmese, who have a genetic predisposition.'

'Oh. Is that why she collapsed?'

'Yes. Her insulin levels were dangerously low. I gave her a shot, and she's responded well to that, as you can see.'

'She seems fine now,' said Oliver, watching as Lala stretched and purred happily as Zara rubbed her belly.

'Hmm, well, she's not. She needs to go on a strict diet and

have insulin injections twice a day,' Dr Joshi said. 'And *no treats*. I'm not sure what you've been feeding her, but it has to stop.' Dr Joshi wagged a finger at her, and Zara felt embarrassed that she was being taken to task. *Bloody Erin.*

Dr Joshi went on to outline Lala's treatment in more detail and showed her how to perform the injections. Soon Zara and Oliver were piling back into a cab, with the cat cage between them, and Zara grasping a paper bag containing syringes and vials, a diet plan and the receipt for a hefty vet bill which she was trying not to think about.

'She'll be OK,' said Oliver, taking Zara's silence for worry. 'You'll make sure of it.'

She grunted. 'Hopefully. At the moment I feel like the worst cat owner in the world.'

'Don't be so hard on yourself. You're a great PT. Look at what you did for me, you've worked wonders.'

'No, I worked a miracle,' said Zara deadpan. Oliver laughed.

At the flat, Oliver helped her transfer Lala inside, the weight of the cat cage needing both of them to carry it.

'Ooof, lucky I've got some muscles now,' Oliver quipped. 'Otherwise you'd be doing the heavy lifting.'

'Haha.'

When Lala was settled in her cat basket in the kitchen with her favourite catnip toy, Zara realised she now needed to play host since Oliver had helped her so much.

'Um, do you want a cup of tea? And we should have some Jammie Dodgers left if Lala hasn't eaten them all.'

'Sure, thanks.' Oliver sat at the kitchen table and looked around as Zara made the tea.

'Nice flat. Strange I'm seeing it now after I've broken up with Erin.'

Zara turned and looked at him. 'Ah, yeah, I forgot you've never been here. How come?'

'Because of you.'

'Me?'

'Yes, the whole PT–client thing. Erin said you didn't want to cross any boundaries. And it would've been weird if we were ... you know, in her room.' Oliver cleared his throat. 'So we always went to mine.'

'Oh, right.'

Zara brought the cups of tea over to the table and plonked an open packet of biscuits down. 'Not too many. Don't want you ending up at the vet's,' she said lightly.

Oliver grinned and took a biscuit.

'So since we're on the subject of Erin. I did want to talk to you actually,' he said.

Zara nibbled on a biscuit. 'Oh?'

'First of all I want to apologise for my behaviour at the gym that day. You were right to call me out on it. But you should know that even though I was acting like an idiot, I wasn't cheating on Erin.'

'Oh no,' Zara said hurriedly. 'You've got nothing to apologise for. I was totally out of line.'

Oliver looked at her, amused. 'You should take the apology.'

'OK, then, thanks. I accept your apology.'

'Good. And secondly …' Oliver stared into her eyes, and Zara took a big gulp of tea. She suddenly felt nervous, like this conversation was headed into deep and meaningful territory. But Oliver just said, 'Have you seen Lachlan lately?'

'Lachlan?' Zara made a non-committal noise. 'No, I haven't spoken to him since Erin's birthday dinner. Why?'

'Uh … I'm not sure if you know, but he does cocaine. He was snorting it in the bathroom in the restaurant. I didn't see it firsthand but some other guy that was in there told me. I thought I should mention it as it was a bit out of line. No pun intended.'

Zara sighed. 'I didn't know that about him but I'm not really surprised. I'll add it to the list of everything else I don't like about him. If he ever resurfaces, I'll give him the flick. Thanks for telling me.'

'So what now?'

'Back to the drawing board, I guess.'

'No guys at the gym you've got your eye on?' Oliver asked

innocently.

'Hmm,' replied Zara, not wanting to fall into that trap. 'None that I can think of.'

'Oh,' Oliver said, sounding faintly disappointed. He drained the rest of his tea. 'Well, I should get going. I don't really want to be here if Erin shows up.'

'She doesn't normally get home until six, but I take your point. I'll see you out.'

'Bye, Lala,' Oliver said. 'Hope you feel better soon.'

'Thanks for helping me with her,' said Zara as she led them to the front door. 'It was really nice of you.'

'Anytime.' There was a tenderness in his voice and Zara kicked herself for being too nonchalant in the kitchen. She needed to keep the conversation going. This day had been an anomaly. The likelihood of hanging out with him again was zero if she didn't make an effort to connect.

'So I guess I'll see you at the gym?'

'Yeah. Maybe we could go for a coffee or something ...' Oliver was leaning against the door jamb and looking down at her enquiringly. He was definitely lingering now, she thought.

'That would be nice.'

Oliver smiled and reading the mood, reached in to give Zara a friendly hug and a kiss on the cheek. But he got the timing wrong as she'd angled her face towards him and he ended up kissing her full on the lips. He pulled back immediately, his face twisting in a grimace. 'Sorry! That wasn't meant to happen!'

Zara laughed at his expression. 'Is it that terrible to kiss me?'

'Of course not. It's just, I shouldn't have …'

'Yes, you should have,' she said seriously. 'And if you don't do it again, then I'm definitely going to make a little note on your record.'

And with that encouragement, Oliver had no trouble kissing her again.

Chapter 30

OLIVER

The only problem with being a 'satellite' office was that periodically Oliver's company would send one of the bigwigs on a tour to spread a particular corporate communication across all the workplaces to make sure that everyone was getting the same message. Oliver was convinced it was an excuse to justify demanding that everyone came into the office a certain number of days per week. Because of the presence of a senior manager, everybody had made an effort with their dress, even those that made a point of not wanting to play those sorts of games. The official dress code was smart casual, but they weren't customer facing, so they could get away with anything.

Sam had opted for a nice white blouse which contrasted nicely with her complexion, while Toby had on his best black metal t-shirt featuring some sort of demonic figure playing a guitar. Oliver suspected it was also probably the only clean one Toby had. Oliver, on the other hand, was wearing a blue-collared shirt under a smart blazer. He'd arrived in the auditorium first and found a seat, but by the time the other two arrived, there was no room on his row, so they sat behind him, the seats being staggered so that they weren't just staring at the back of his head. They had a few minutes as the auditorium continued to fill up.

Sam gave him a nudge. 'How are things going with Erin?'

He half turned in his seat, answering her over his shoulder. 'Ah ... Erin and I broke up, actually.'

'Oh no, I'm really sorry to hear that!' She lowered her voice and leaned closer. 'What happened?' Toby leaned forward too.

Oliver shrugged. 'It was for the best; it was mutual.'

Toby opened his mouth. Oliver continued before he could say anything.

'It really *was* mutual. We both wanted different things. So it worked out well. And I kind of like her flatmate anyway.'

Sam blinked in surprise. Toby guffawed.

'Big mistake, man. If you liked the flatmate, you should have gotten them both drunk and then boom! Threesome! Try before you buy, man! What if this new chick is a lousy lay? Better to be able to compare and contrast. And anyway, do you even know if this new girl likes you? You might be giving up a sure thing for a maybe. That's not smart.'

Oliver looked over his other shoulder at Toby. He wasn't sure if Toby meant half the things he said, sometimes he said provocative things just to incite outrage.

'Well ...' Oliver said.

Toby frowned. Sam got it pretty quickly. 'Does she like you?' Oliver twisted the other way and tried not to grin like the Cheshire Cat.

'Well ... we kissed last night,' he allowed in a near whisper. Their conversation had pretty much been eaten by the background noise of an audience waiting for a show, so there was little chance of it being heard by very many people.

Sam and Toby both clapped him on the shoulders in congratulations.

Toby paused as he had a thought. 'Hang on, are you sure you're not just on the rebound?'

Oliver's neck was feeling the strain of twisting one way and then the other. 'We weren't really together that long, to tell the truth,' he managed, 'and I knew Zara before I met Erin.'

'Awwww, that's so sweet,' Sam cooed.

'So it was more like getting some strange before a long-term relationship? Like it, like it. Respect.'

'Some what? Strange?' Great, now Sam and Toby were talking, and Oliver had to twist 270 degrees to look at each one in turn.

'Strange: you know, sex with someone you haven't had sex with before. Strange.'

Sam looked flummoxed at the term as Oliver continued his defence.

'No, no, that's not it at all. I was just able to finally act on my feelings for Zara.'

'Well, as I said, a wasted opportunity. When I get a girlfriend, she's going to be totally up for threesomes all the time.'

'Yeah, I don't know how likely that will be,' said Sam with a sidelong glance at Toby.

Oliver gave them a look, Sam over one shoulder with a light shade directly overhead, making her look like she had a halo, while Toby over the other shoulder with his demonic shirt and darker commentary making him more of a devil's advocate. Then the guest speaker walked up to the front of the stage, and their meeting started.

It was a rest day from the gym, so after work, Oliver headed straight home. All the way there he tortured himself, trying to figure out how long to leave it before getting in touch with Zara. He didn't want to come across as needy, but she was the only thing he had been thinking about since 'The Kiss' had happened. To distract himself, he reached out to Mark to see if he was available for a chat.

Mark was obviously using his phone, the angle of the video being an unflattering upward shot making his head look like a thumb wearing earbuds. Skyscrapers loomed in the background and street noise competed with the sounds of Mark's breathing. 'Yo, Oliver, my man! How are things going?'

'Good. Where are you?'

'New York. Work has got me over here for a conference. *Hey buddy, I'm walking here*. Ha! I've always wanted to say that.'

'Be careful: the traffic doesn't muck around. Hey, I wanted to talk to you about something.'

'Cool. What's up?'

'I've liked a girl for a while now, and last night I kissed her.'

'What? That's brilliant! *Excuse you—watch where you're walking, dipshit*. Ah, hang on. Did she kiss you back? Or did she run away? Are the cops coming? Are you in trouble?'

'Dickhead. No, she kissed me back.'

'Who is she?'

'You remember how I was working out with a personal trainer?'

'I think so: the petite blonde?'

'Yeah. Zara. I've kind of liked her for a long time now, and one thing led to another and ... yeah.'

'Well done! That's really good! Just last night then? So was it just a kiss then?'

'A really, really good kiss. Man, I get all dreamy just thinking about it.'

'What, are you a sixteen-year-old girl? "Dreamy" he says! I thought you had a girlfriend? What happened to … Fenella?'

'Erin?'

'Yeah, Erin. Are you cheating on her? You don't seem the type. *You got a death wish, buddy? The light's green!*'

'No, I broke things off with her. Oh, actually, technically, she broke up with me, but I was going to do it at the same time, so it's kind of a—'

The street noise suddenly silenced as the background changed to the interior of a hotel lobby, and Mark's volume lowered. 'You really are a sixteen-year-old, aren't you? It doesn't matter who broke up with who. So you broke up with your girlfriend and now you've finally got the girl that you wanted all along. That sounds like a win to me. Congratulations. Was there something more or are you just bragging?'

'Well, I guess the only little issue is that Zara is Erin's flatmate.'

Mark stopped, rubbed his chin and sucked in his breath. 'Oooh. That's going to be awkward, man. You better clean your flat because you won't be able to spend any time at

Zara's place. Just in case you bump into Erin on the way to the bathroom.'

'It was an amicable breakup, and we're both adults. I think we should be fine.'

'Hey, take a little bit of advice from someone who's been there and done that? Hide the scissors. And the knives. Anything which can cut or pierce. You say it was amicable and that's great in the cold light of the day, but after a few pinot noirs and in the dark on the way to the bathroom, she may decide that she doesn't like your new love rubbed in her face and she might decide, purely as a result of the alcohol, you understand, to make a few adjustments to your body vis-à-vis which bits are joined to which other bits. Leaving you with an unfortunate piercing that you didn't ask for and wanting to just get to the bathroom and empty your bladder. So yeah. Get someone in to give the apartment a deep clean and maybe someone in once a month to keep on top of it.'

'I'm capable of keeping my flat clean, Mark.'

'Sure. It's been a while for you, my man. "Boy clean" and "girl clean" are two different things. If you want to stay together, it might be an idea to put some attention in that area.'

'Fine, OK. A cleaner. Anything else? Any advice from the big Romeo?'

'When was the kiss? Last night? When are you seeing her

next?'

'We sometimes see each other at the gym. In fact, I think she will be there tomorrow. Today was a rest day for me. I don't want to scare her off, but I really, really want to talk to her.'

Mark had obviously found a couch in the lobby. 'OK, there are a diverse range of opinions about how long you should wait to talk to someone after a physical breakthrough. Usually, I'm dealing with how long after sleeping with someone, but we can apply that to a first kiss as well. The theory is that you should wait a couple of days to keep them on edge and make them wonder if it meant as much to you as it did them. But it sounds like it means a lot to you. Another theory is that you should outwait them: the first to get in touch loses.'

Oliver frowned. 'And what do you think?'

'I usually text them while I'm on the way home.'

'Wow, that's soon!'

'Yeah, stuff the rules. Sometimes it's the gentle letdown after a one-night stand. Sometimes it's a little more open.'

'So you never ghost anyone?'

'Sure, you can do that. But it's a little disrespectful. Surely you owe closure to someone that you've just been intimate with? It costs practically nothing.'

'So if I rang her tonight, that wouldn't be bad?'

'Dude, you're pining after her like a teenager. I take it that you didn't feel like this when you got together with Fenella?'

'Fenella? Oh, Erin? No.' Oliver considered that a little longer. 'No, I didn't. I think I was just caught up in the fact that someone liked me. Anyone. That was nice after so long. But ...'

'No connection? And major connection with this one? Olly, my man. Call her tonight. Talk to her. And, Olly? Remember that Mark is a good name for your first kid. Just saying!'

Chapter 31

ZARA

After Oliver left, Zara had launched into extreme tidying mode. Something she always did when she had too much energy to sit still and she had things on her mind. But it had worked because she'd successfully managed to wrestle her conscience into submission—it was just a kiss, it didn't mean anything—mainly because of her guilt about Erin. You shouldn't snog your flatmate's ex-boyfriend. Not if you wanted to keep living with them.

She'd zoned out, watching a reality show on Netflix to keep from going over and over 'The Kiss' in her mind. Zara didn't register that Erin was home until she was standing in front of her in the lounge.

'You didn't message me!' she said, sounding annoyed.

'Ah no, sorry! I forgot. There was a lot going on. She's home, though.' Zara indicated the sleeping Lala at the foot of the couch.

'I can see that.' Erin looked like she wanted to chat further, so Zara turned off the telly.

'Let's talk in the kitchen so we don't wake her. She's had a stressful day.'

'So have I,' grumbled Erin, going through to the other room. She slung her handbag on the back of the closest chair while Zara flicked on the kettle. She turned and saw that Erin was sitting in the exact place where Oliver had been an hour ago. A vision of him kissing her in the entranceway flew into her mind and she pushed it aside, guilt rising. Keeping her back to Erin, she furtively rinsed her and Oliver's dirty mugs and put them in the dishwasher. 'How did the presentation go?'

'Badly because I was worried about Lala. Then you didn't message, so I thought the worst. Is she OK?'

Zara brought two fresh mugs down from the cupboard. 'Yes and no. She's got diabetes, so I'm going to have to monitor exactly what she eats. Plus give her injections twice a day.' She resisted the urge to add, 'And it's all your fault.'

'Shit. That's not good. Sorry you had to cope with all that alone. In hindsight, I should've just said I wasn't well and moved my presentation to another day.'

'I wasn't alone. Oliver was there,' Zara said without thinking.

'*Oliver?*' Zara cringed at Erin's accusing tone. 'Why did

he get involved?'

'He, er, saw I was upset and offered to come with me.'

'Huh. I bet he did.'

'What's that supposed to mean?'

'Nothing.' Zara didn't push it but silently brought their tea over to the table. She didn't bring out the Jammie Dodgers because Oliver had ended up finishing the packet. 'Stress eating,' he'd said, 'it's allowed when you've had a shock.'

'So why didn't you tell me you guys had broken up?'

Erin frowned and sipped her tea. 'He mentioned that, did he?'

'Well, yeah. Is there a reason he shouldn't have?'

'I guess not. I just ... I've been doing some thinking in the Cotswolds. It's really lovely there, by the way; you should come with me next time.'

'Thinking about what exactly?' Zara enquired.

'About me and Oliver. Perhaps I was too hasty breaking up with him. Maybe we should give it another go now we've both had time to think.'

Zara's heart sank. 'I thought it was a mutual break-up, though. That you both wanted different things?'

Erin regarded Zara stonily over the top of her mug. 'Sounds like you know all about it. Did he give you a blow-by-blow account of our conversation in the cafe?'

'Of course not. Only just what I said.'

'What happened after the vet's?' asked Erin suddenly.

Zara couldn't very well lie to her face. 'Oh, er, Oliver helped me bring Lala into the flat. Then I, um, offered him a cup of tea.'

Erin narrowed her eyes. Zara shifted uncomfortably under her scrutiny. *Just stop asking questions,* she thought. But Erin had smelt a rat.

'So then he left?'

'Pretty much.'

Zara's cheeks were on fire, she couldn't help it. 'The Kiss' was vivid in her mind. Oliver gently pushing her hair back from her face and his lips slowly inching towards hers. When he'd kissed her properly, there was no awkwardness. They'd made out like a couple of teenagers, hungry for each other, right there on the doorstep. It had been awesome.

Erin stared at her suspiciously, noting her discomfort. 'Something happened, didn't it? You might as well tell me.'

Zara swallowed. 'Well, he, um, we kissed. Just when he was leaving. But it was nothing. It didn't mean anything. I'm really sorry.'

She saw Erin's face blanch and her lips tighten. Zara braced herself for the explosion. But Erin did something even worse than yell at her. She got up slowly, unhooked her handbag from the chair and silently walked out of the kitchen. Moments later, Zara heard the door to the flat open and close, then Erin's Fiat fire into life and take off down the street.

A couple of weeks later, Zara was alone in the gym lunchroom eating her chicken salad when Jase came in, also alone. *Great*, she thought, *just what I need.*

'Zee,' he said, giving her a nod.

'Jase,' she replied. She thought that would be it for communication, so she picked up her phone to check Spare Room. But after he'd made his protein shake, she was surprised when he sat down opposite her.

'How's it going?' he asked after swallowing a mouthful of green liquid. Zara put her phone down on the table. Might as well be sociable since he seemed interested in talking.

'Fine. How's it going with you? Still with Amber?'

'Nah. That's over. Has been for a while.'

'Oh, sorry.'

Jase shrugged and noticed the app open on her phone. 'Looking for a new flat?'

'Yeah.' Zara didn't feel the need to go into details. That she was now sleeping on a pullout couch in her mum's lounge with boxes of her stuff piled up in the corner. Erin had come back after a long drive and decided it was time she moved out. She'd given her a week's notice. It was an awkward shitty situation but what could Zara do about it? At least she'd told her the truth.

As Amanda had pointed out, she was better off at her mum's than living with Erin. At first she couldn't really see that she was, but after the haze of disbelief and upset at being kicked out had worn off, she was inclined to agree. She was now in Zone One, so she was closer to work and the Tube fare was less; plus her mother and June were helping her to look after Lala, and she could trust them with her diet—there was no chance of that now with Erin. Lala was doing so much better, and she was definitely on the road to health, even if it involved Kate performing cat reiki sessions …

'Anything in particular you're looking for?' asked Jase, taking another slurp of green goo.

'Zone One if possible, and they have to like cats. But other than that, I'm not fussy.'

'Hmm, I think Joanna is looking for a flatmate. I seem to recall her asking around about it a few days ago. She's in Zone One.'

'Really?'

'Yeah. But she may have found someone. You should get on to it pronto.'

Zara perked up. Joanna was a PT who had started around the same time as she had. They were friendly if they ran into each other but Joanna started training sessions at the crack of dawn because she had another side gig. Their schedules never matched because she was always leaving the gym when Zara was coming in. *That could be a good thing,* thought Zara. *I'd practically have the flat to myself.*

'Thanks,' she told Jase. 'I'll grab her card right now and give her a text.'

'No probs.'

Zara picked up her phone and her empty salad container feeling more upbeat about the flat situation.

'Zee?'

'Yes?' said Zara distractedly, heading to the sink to rinse her container.

'Since things are over with Amber, I wondered if you might want to ... you know ...' He trailed off, seeming a little embarrassed.

Zara stared at him, a bit gobsmacked. 'Hookup?'

'Well, yeah,' Jase said expectantly.

God, he had a nerve. 'Sorry, Jase, I'm kind of interested in someone,' she said.

'Oh, sure. Who is it? One of the new PTs?' Jase didn't even look that worried that she'd said no, Zara noted.

'No, he's not a PT,' she said. 'See you later, Jase.'

Zara walked out into the gym, heading for the wall of perspex slots where each of the PTs had their business cards and profile sheets. She located Joanna's business card and sent her a text asking if she was still searching for a flatmate, and if so, she was keen.

Looking over at the row of treadmills, she spotted a lone guy jogging on the one by the window. It was just before the lunch rush, so the gym was pretty empty at this time. *Early bird*, she thought, smiling and strolled in that direction. The treadmill next to him was free, so she pushed GO and started a five-minute walk to warm up.

Oliver swivelled his head to see who it was and gave her a big grin. 'Hey!'

She smiled at him. 'Hey yourself.'

'Got a client?'

'Not until two.'

'Ah. So just a little light workout until then?'

'Yeah. I was actually thinking that I might enter the half marathon too. If you wanted a training buddy, that is. We could spur each other on.'

'I'd like that. A lot,' he said, nodding.

'It wouldn't be a PT–client relationship, though.'

'Hmm, makes sense. Well, not after last night.' Oliver smirked, and Zara blushed. They'd been out on their first proper date since she'd moved to her mum's place. Oliver had taken her to a local pub for dinner and drinks, and they'd ended up going back to his place afterwards. One thing had led to another, and she'd experienced the full effects of just how fit Oliver had become. His stamina in bed was impressive. That was one exercise she was definitely giving him top marks for.

She coughed. 'So yeah, that was fun.'

Oliver laughed. 'It was! Funnily enough, I was actually going to ask you if you wanted to train together when we were in the pub last night, but you seduced me before I had the chance,' he said, starting to puff as he'd put his treadmill on rather a steep incline.

'I seduced you?' Zara increased her speed keeping pace with him. 'I think you'll find it was the other way round.'

'Oh no,' said Oliver. 'I'm not in the habit of behaving inappropriately in pubs. Well, not after "the incident" at the Hat and Tun, at least.'

'I think you better start from the beginning and tell me everything,' said Zara, settling into a comfortable jog.

'Well, OK, but the thing to remember here was that it was totally *not* my fault ...'

Chapter 32

OLIVER

'How many steps?'

'Three hundred and eighty-two.'

'Three hundred …!'

'... and eighty-two.'

They stood at the base of a steep incline leading from the sea level of the train station to the town on the hill. Concrete rather than the red stone of Petra, and a uniform series of switchbacks rather than the meandering path up to the Monastery. Zara looked up at him, and he wrapped his arms around her and gazed at the stairs beyond. Easy.

They'd changed the flight and hotel booking with minimal issues. There was a small fee for the air tickets to change the name and the destination airport, and upon investigation, Oliver found that the hotel booking was completely refundable. They had splurged on a taxi to get to Stansted, even in the early hours of the morning, finding the conversation flowing very easily.

'How's the flat working out?' Oliver asked.

'It's great,' Zara replied. 'Joanna is hardly there, and she listens to me when I say that she can't feed Lala. I'm tempted to get Erin to pay for her treatment.'

Oliver shook his head. 'Probably not the best approach. I'm no lawyer, and my knowledge of pet health law is pretty sketchy, but it might be expensive to discover that you don't have a leg to stand on. And pet medical bills are sooo expensive! Did I tell you about the family cat when I was growing up?'

Zara shook her head.

'We lived on a cul-de-sac, but there was one neighbour who would drive a little too fast around the corner and then coast into his driveway. He was a young guy and there weren't any kids in the neighbourhood, so he figured it was safe enough.'

Zara frowned. 'Why did he coast the rest of the way?'

'The road was on a bit of a hill, and it was almost semi industrial, so no traffic and good camber on the streets, so a bit of a thrill. Or something, I don't know. Anyway we had a cat, Jester; he must have been ten years old and a real miserable bastard. The size of a racoon and similar markings. But an indoor cat. We had this cat flap in the back door but he was too big for it, so he would only wander out the door whenever anyone came in or out. That was fine, we just made sure he was inside overnight. Otherwise, he would make a din when he finally decided he wanted to come inside. At midnight.

'And one night in the height of summer, nobody had seen Jester. And we didn't think anything of it. But come the morning we heard this pitiful mewing coming from under the house. And Dad opened the hatch that led under the house and out came this hobbling cat. His front leg was mangled and he had all this gravel stuck to him and he was in a bad way. We took him to the vet, and they said that they wouldn't be able to save the leg but that they could amputate it and try and get the gravel out of him, and the whole thing would cost three grand.'

'Wow, that's a lot of money.'

'Yeah. I listened to my stepmum and dad talking about it. She said that because she couldn't have any kids that she thought of Jester as her kid. That's why she let him get to that size. Anyway, she told Dad in no uncertain terms that she wanted him to find the money for the operation. So I know that pet care is expensive.'

'Don't leave me hanging! What happened to the cat? Was he OK?'

Oliver looked uncomfortable. 'Truth? He was never the same after the op and had a miserable existence. They had to get him put down not long after.'

'Oh no!'

'Yeah, nobody talked about it after that. And nobody complained that we didn't go on holiday that year. And we got a pair of kittens not long after.'

Stansted wasn't Oliver's favourite of London's airports. In fact, he shared an oft-repeated complaint that Stansted and Luton shouldn't really be considered London airports. But after an uneventful checking-in and boarding, they were taxiing, ready to take off.

'Are you a nervous flier?' asked Zara.

'Not nervous, no. I've done a fair bit of flying, but I tell you what is good. Losing the belly makes getting on and off easier and the seat belt more comfortable. Especially on those long-haul flights. Damn near thought I'd be cut in half with my flight to Amman.'

The one thing Oliver missed about changing their destination was the view of Venice from the air, seeing the islands and the canals and the terracotta roofs would have been awesome, but instead they landed in Pisa, which consisted of a brief glimpse of the beach followed by a couple of minutes of forest and then the airport. A ten-minute bus ride got them into the town and then ninety minutes later, they were hopping off the train at Riomaggiore, the first of the five towns of the Cinque Terre.

They paused for lunch at a cafe before exploring the town,

which admittedly didn't take long. The pastel colours of the houses were in stark contrast to the drabness of the grey rock on which they were built. And while the town was draped on a hill and met the brilliant blue Mediterranean, there was no beach per se, just a stone ramp leading into the water as the buildings of the town loomed overhead. The town shops and cafes were higher up on the hill and surprisingly only had views of each other across the pedestrian road, like being in a canyon and only being able to see the opposite wall of the canyon rather than the grand vista. They briefly visited the castle on the hill before leaving for the next town and were very glad that they did.

Oliver stood behind Zara, and she leaned into him as they surveyed the sight of the Mediterranean stretching out in front of them, the colourful buildings nestled around the sea ramp below them to the left and the other towns hidden by the headlands to their right. This was more like it!

The trek between Riomaggiore and the next town took no time at all, although again, the pedestrian walkway from rail station to town was through an enclosed tunnel which led them up the inside of the hill to the top, popping them out into the well-paved streets with the town buildings looming on both sides. While there were boats parked on the road outside the cafes and restaurants, there were even fewer facilities to access the water here—some sort of boat winch in effect to get the boats into the water but so many rocks making access dangerous. Oliver and Zara didn't spend too much time in town, heading on for a slightly longer leg to Corniglia. As Oliver put it, 'It sounds like a cross between a farmer and an ancient Roman emperor.'

The walk was almost down to sea level, carved into the cliff face and in parts protected from falling boulders with wire netting. The turquoise Mediterranean was a constant distraction to the left, and the picturesque town poised on the hilltop ahead of them. Corniglia, the middle of the five towns, was the only one perched on top of the hill, and even though Italy and Jordan were very different, the sight of so many steps in the glaring sunlight brought back the bad memories of the ascent to the Monastery.

The half marathon training had been going well—and that reflected in their relationship going well also. Oliver had made sure that Zara was regularly pampered. He was getting quite good with the massage oil and digging in his thumbs to release the deepest knots in her muscles. He'd always stop when she gasped when he went deep on a particularly problematic area, but she would always tell him to carry on. 'Harder,' she'd say.

Overall, the results were showing. Oliver was sure that they could hike the complete distance of the Cinque Terre from south to north and back again in one day, but then what would they do with the rest of the weekend? Besides, he wanted to enjoy their time together. And the ability to conquer steps like the ones in front of them.

They were momentarily held up by a mother corralling four kids, and Oliver experienced a brief flashback to the wedding they'd gone to. Thank heaven Zara wasn't quite ready for kids. He knew that Erin had been right and there was no way he was ready for them just yet, but he was happy in growing in that direction with Zara if that's what they decided they wanted. No pressure.

The kids seemed determined to stand two abreast despite the mother's best efforts, so Oliver and Zara just ducked under the safety bars and leapfrogged them in the switchbacks. And then there was nothing between them and the top except probably two hundred stairs in constant zigzags.

Zara wasn't even breathing hard, and it didn't take Oliver long to recover his breath at the top, and then they continued on the path into the town proper. It was strange that they were so high above sea level, and yet there was so little to see, just the road, embankments and houses. Oliver figured that Cinque Terre made you work for the views. He was proved right when they made their way off the main road and found a lovely lookout point. They could see all the way along the coast from where they had come and a fair way to where they were going. And it looked gorgeous.

'I'm all sweaty,' Zara said as he came up behind her to put his arms around her.

'I don't care,' Oliver said, nuzzling her cheek. 'I love you.'

She murmured something back.

'What was that? I didn't quite hear you.'

She turned and looked up at him. 'I love you too. You make me happy.'

He leaned down and gave her a gentle kiss. Some time later they decided to move on, heading back to the main road and through the narrow alleys of the town.

'It's too early for dinner, do you want a snack? Or can you wait a little longer?' asked Zara.

'Oh, lunch wasn't long ago. I can last a bit longer,' Oliver replied.

Zara stopped outside a shop lit from within, a yellow glow stark against the surrounding stone walls. A cartoon sketch above the door featured the dirty face of some kid enjoying a chocolate confectionery, and a chalkboard proclaimed the flavours of gelato and other desserts on offer within.

'What about something to tide us over til dinner? Crepes? An ice cream? They do cannoli?' Zara asked.

Oliver grinned at her. 'You had me at ice cream.'

THE END

Keep Reading

If you enjoyed *You Had Me at Ice Cream*,
check out Chapter One of Angela's rom-com
I'll Meet You in Florence. (TW: this one is spicier!)

Opposites attract when Jenna scores a house sit in
Hampstead Heath and falls for the owner's stepson,
Seth, who lives in the back garden.
Their chance encounter in London heats up in Italy
when he decides to follow her to Florence.

Available on Amazon and Kindle Unlimited

I'll Meet You in Florence – Chapter 1

'Have you got that, Jenna?' Whipping my head around, I find India Carver staring at me—pointedly. Whoops.

I'm supposed to be listening to her quick-fire explanation about the solar power. But I've been distracted by a sweeping black marble staircase, the super high ceilings looming above and the sheer number of crystal chandeliers. I can count at least five from where I'm standing.

And the electronics. Oh my God. Nothing has a simple switch. The whole house is digitally operated from a phone app. No wonder I've spaced out.

'I'll text you the link to the app and you can download it,' India says. 'It's quite simple. But we should have a run-through before I go, otherwise you won't have electricity. And I don't want to have to field calls about it while I'm on holiday.'

I nod gratefully. 'Thanks.'

Erk. That's put me in my place.

This Victorian mansion in Hampstead is enormous and it's caught me off guard. The website listing didn't have any photos of the house, only the cat, so I was expecting an average-sized semi with the usual two or three bedrooms. Not a seven-bedroom, fifteen-foot ceiling, five chandelier affair.

The owners are just a couple rattling around in all this space. They must be either stonkingly rich from their day jobs or have inherited a lot of money. From the snippets of what India's been telling me, I've managed to piece together that Drew Carver, her husband, is a music producer and that she owns an organic skincare business. I haven't been able to place her age. She could be anywhere between thirty-five and fifty-five if botox injections are involved. There has been no mention of kids either—toddlers or teenagers—which would have been an instant age marker.

India leads the way up the marble staircase, then glides down the dark-wood parquet hallway in her pink leather house slippers. She's asked me to take my shoes off, so I'm skidding in my ankle socks. She gestures at doors right and left, announcing their purpose 'our room… main bathroom… Drew's study… media lounge… zoo room…'

Zoo room? That sounds worrying. As far as I know, there's just the cat to look after. My ears prick for any squeaks or squawks that might suggest a menagerie of exotic animals. Sometimes owners also try to slip in friends' dogs, so you have to be on your guard. But there are no suspicious noises that I can hear coming from the room.

We continue until she pauses outside a room at the far end of the hall and glances back at me to check if I'm keeping up.

Her blonde hair swishes across her cheekbone, then swings into place. We both have shoulder-length bobs with layered fringes. Unlike my straight golden-brown locks, which I trim myself because I can't afford a haircut at the moment, her cut is immaculate. Almost as if her stylist has used a ruler to make sure every hair on her head is the correct length.

'This is the largest of our guest rooms and the only one on the top floor. But you can choose one of the others downstairs if you'd like to be closer to the kitchen,' she says. I recall the earlier part of our grand tour in which five guest bedrooms were mentioned. At least I've remembered something.

India leads the way into the guest room, and I gape. The walls are pink. But not any old pink. Luscious strawberry gelato pink. An oak four-poster bed features white satin bedding and a gossamer canopy. On the floor is a faux zebra-skin rug. The black-and-white theme is matched by framed prints of iconic movie stars dotted around the walls; Audrey Hepburn, Marilyn Monroe, Grace Kelly. It's a Disney bedroom for grown-up princesses who go designer shopping in Knightsbridge.

'It's *fantastic*,' I breathe, forgetting it's gauche to show one's excitement when shown around an upmarket house sit. 'Like medieval meets modern with a nod to retro.'

'Yes, that's exactly what I was going for. Drew thought it was too much but I went with my instincts.'

'No, it totally works!'

India looks approving. 'What do you do again, Jenna? I don't think you said in your profile.'

'Oh, I'm an interior decorator,' I say, after a pause. I don't tend to mention this because then owners want to know why I'm house sitting and start asking awkward questions; and it's my foot-in-the-door system to win clients. This is how it works. I subtly rearrange the furniture or accessories in a room as if on a whim. Then, when the owners get back and exclaim 'Oh, this looks different but much better!' I casually mention I'm an interior decorator. If they say something like, 'I've been wanting to redecorate' or 'I have a friend who needs an interior decorator', then I have an in.

But advising someone on the best shade of beige carpet for a one-bedroom flat in Wandsworth is small fry. Taking on a room in a house like this is exactly what I'm after if I want to raise my profile.

However, India doesn't leap at the chance of hiring me or suggest she has a friend in need of my services. 'It has a nice outlook over the garden, much like our room,' she says, changing the subject. She flings opens the mullioned window and I peer over her shoulder. 'Wow!' I exclaim before I can stop myself.

The garden is at least an acre; landscaped lawn, clipped box hedges and raised flower beds full of pink roses. Methinks the lady of the manor has ordered a themed garden to be created in her honour. Over to the left, I spy a decent-sized swimming pool twinkling blue in the sunlight. There's also a lovely wooden cabana with a straw thatch roof and white lattice loungers. Situated behind the pool is a glossy black shipping container with a sliding door, windows and a little wooden deck. The garden shed, I assume. A property this size probably needs a lot of hoes and hedge clippers and other… implements.

I'm about to comment on it, but India says she'll show me the kitchen next so we can have a cup of tea and go over the app for the solar electrics. 'I need to order my taxi to meet Drew at his office in Hammersmith,' she remarks looking at her watch. 'We're going to Heathrow from there. Rush hour traffic will be positively hellish. I wish we had a private helicopter. I might ask him about getting one.' I almost let out an amused chuckle but then realise—she's not joking.

Downstairs, I'm greeted with yet another revelation, the kitchen of my dreams. It's a new extension, India tells me. Glass bi-fold doors open out onto an upper-level garden patio. There are three skylights. A polished brass mixer tap and an oversized sink are fitted into a white marble counter. The walls are lined with sleek high-gloss black cabinets. The glass-top kitchen table could seat twenty people. It's all a bit overwhelming.

India is dying to show me the chrome kettle. 'It's clever, we ordered it from the US,' she says. 'Watch this.'

She holds up her palms and claps twice. Soon, there's the sound of boiling water, and steam rises from the spout.

'You clap once to turn it off. That's the only drawback. If you forget, it boils dry, and it's game over for the kettle. When we first got it, we were clapping like mad things and ended up with cups of tea for Africa. Sephy thought we were potty, didn't you Sephy, darling?'

Sephy (aka Persephone) is their grey fluffy Persian and the reason they need a housesitter. She's just made an appearance in the kitchen through the cat door and chirrups at India, no doubt thinking she's going to get an early dinner. India picks her up and buries her face in the soft fur, causing the cat to squirm. 'Isn't she adorable?' says India to me. Sephy swipes a sharp-clawed paw, narrowly missing India's smooth unblemished cheek. I don't ask if I can have a cuddle, those claws look lethal.

After herbal tea and solar electrics 101, India shows me the garden. Stepping out through the doors and onto the red-brick patio, we stand there shading our eyes in the glare of the afternoon sun. 'You can get to the pool that way,' she says pointing to some concrete steps.

They lead onto a path which winds down through low shrubbery and ends at the pool. Hot rays beat down on my shoulders and the water looks cool and refreshing. I haven't been for a swim once this summer, so I'm glad I packed my bikini on the off-chance they had a pool.

'Your shipping container garden shed is on trend,' I comment, trying to sound in the know.

'Oh, it's not a garden shed. That's Seth's studio,' India says airily.

'Seth?' I echo. 'Is he the on-site gardener?'

She gives a short laugh. 'No, he's my stepson.'

What? I glower inside but am careful to make sure it doesn't show on my face. I hate it when house owners do this. You think you're going to be alone, then you find out you're also babysitting a teenager and their teenage friends. Before you know it, there's an all-night drinking session underway.

'Um, right. How old is Seth?'

'He's twenty-six.'

OK, so not a teenager.

'Why can't he look after Persephone? Is he going away too?' I ask, trying to sound unconcerned.

'Oh no, he's staying here, but he's got his own life and likely to forget.' India sniffs. 'Poor Sephy wouldn't survive if Seth was on cat duty.'

I push down a pang of annoyance.

'Does he come inside to eat?'

India shakes her head. 'It's a self-contained studio, and he's got his own private entrance in the adjoining lane. He nips out to M&S or orders takeaways,' she explains. 'Most of the time I forget he's around. Drew goes down there periodically to check on him to make sure he's still alive.'

'But don't worry,' she says, seeing my eyebrows raise, 'he likes to keep to himself. We've told him we're getting a house sitter. Even though he knows you're here, he won't bother you.'

Well, if that's the case, my shoulders relax and I breathe more easily. It's still fine. I don't have to worry about babysitting someone or having them walk in when I'm doing a bit of subtle knick-knack rearranging. And I can turn a blind eye to any all-night drinking sessions.

'That sounds perfect,' I say, smiling. Excitement bubbles up. *Living in Hampstead for two whole weeks!* I hug myself in glee. Figuratively, of course, India hasn't left the house just yet.

Want to keep reading?
I'll Meet You in Florence is available on
Amazon and Kindle Unlimited

Acknowledgements

Thank you for reading *You Had Me at Ice Cream*, we hope you enjoyed it! If so, we'd be thrilled if you left a review or star rating on Amazon and/or Goodreads.

As always we're grateful for having a team of people to help us on the publishing journey. Thank you to our beta readers: Katie Griffin, Katy Hristova, Lauryn Lambert and Andrew Grenfell for your insightful and honest feedback. Also thanks to Katherine Waghorn for her copyediting and to Kostis Pavlou for his wonderful cover art and patience with all the tweaks!

To receive alerts on upcoming releases,
sign up to our newsletters at:

➜ angelapearse.pub
➜ cglambert.com

Also by

ANGELA PEARSE

I'll Meet You in Florence
The House of Dating Disasters
My Double Life
Travel & Mayhem

C.G. LAMBERT

The Illiterate Prince
The Girl From Wonderland
The Man In The Hotel Ceiling
The Kids Who Lived In A Hole

All books available on Amazon and Kindle Unlimited

About the Authors

ANGELA PEARSE writes quirky romantic comedies which capture the humour of everyday life. A freelance copywriter with an MA in English, Angela enjoys travelling, hiking, cooking, binge-watching Netflix, and reading copious amounts of chick lit. Originally from New Zealand, Angela currently lives in Edinburgh. Visit angelapearse.pub.

C.G. LAMBERT was born the second of seven children and raised in South Auckland, New Zealand. His pre-writing career consisted of applying for whatever job sounded interesting, leading to time as an International Banker, a Music Manager, Web Developer and Analytics Manager. He loves travel (you can read about it at etrip.tips), holds dual citizenship (NZ/UK), a Bachelor of Arts and an MBA. He currently resides in the UNESCO City of Literature, Edinburgh. Visit cglambert.com